CLUB TIMES

For Members' Eyes Only

I've got a secret....

I have to say that this week, I have a little crush on Dr. Sam Walters. He flashed his pearly whites at me in the grocery store as I was fondling fruit. Talk about drop-dead gorgeous! I also caught his nurse, Caitlyn Matthews, standing near the potatoes (carbs don't help anyone, Caitlyn), and she was eyeing the good doctor, too. I like a man who eats from the four food groups.

Thank goodness, Branson Hines is out of our hair. Let's take a collective sigh of relief that Mission Creek is free of another trouble-maker, although I'll bet our small town can stir up a little excitement now and then. What do you think, members?

I must leave you for the time being because of something that needs my undivided attention. You guessed it. I have a bun in the oven, the stork's gonna pay me a visit in eight months, I'm expecting a bundle of joy. Shocked? I bet you thought I was an old biddy... Well, there's still plenty of mileage left in this body. Who's the father, you ask? I'll never tell....

Make sure to keep your eyes and ears open to the goings-on in the wild and wonderful world of Mission Creek. And our very own Lone Star Country Club, the place that makes your heart and soul come alive!

About the Author

Having grown up on an island, **BEVERLY BIRD** loves to write of any locale that does not involve beaches, sand or seagulls. Writing for the LONE STAR COUNTRY CLUB series had the added advantage of getting to "meet" so many other authors who were involved, sharing ideas and inspiration.

BEVERLY BIRD

DOCTOR
SEDUCTION

Silhouette Books

Published by Silhouette Books

America's Publisher of Contemporary Romance

Special thanks and acknowledgment are given to Beverly Bird for her contribution to the LONE STAR COUNTRY CLUB series.

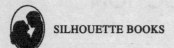

SILHOUETTE BOOKS

ISBN 0-373-61367-9

DOCTOR SEDUCTION

Welcome to the

LONE STAR
LSC
COUNTRY
CLUB
EST. 1923

*Where Texas society reigns supreme—
and appearances are everything.*

*Could danger still lurk behind the doors
of Mission Creek Memorial Hospital?*

Dr. Sam Walters: He had once managed to disguise his powerful attraction for his nurse through his brusque, intimidating manner. But when they were held against their will for three days, this hot-blooded pediatrician's suppressed desires just *couldn't* be denied. Can their tenuous relationship survive the devastating aftershock of their life-altering captivity?

Caitlyn Matthews: She didn't know if she'd ever get past being traumatized by a demented criminal. Nor did the dedicated nurse know how she'd ever be able to reveal to her roguishly charming colleague that their brief yet electric interlude had a most *un*expected result!

Branson Hines: Although the Mission Creek Madman is finally behind bars, he is *still* bent on revenge. Does he have one final ace up his sleeve?

Holly Sinclair: This chipper new hospital cafeteria worker is an all-too-willing confidante to a beleagured Nurse Caitlyn. But what *really* lurks behind her sunny smile?

THE FAMILIES

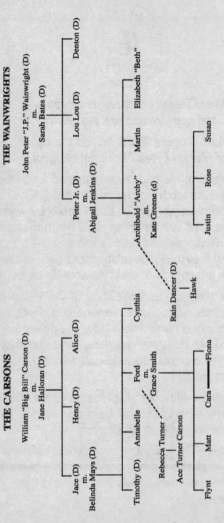

THE CARSONS

William "Big Bill" Carson (D)
m.
Jane Halloran (D)

Jace (D)
m.
Belinda Mays (D)

Henry (D)

Alice (D)

Cynthia

Timothy (D)

Annabelle

Ford
m.
Grace Smith

Rebecca Turner

Ace Turner Carson

Flynt

Matt

Cara — Fiona

THE WAINWRIGHTS

John Peter "J.P." Wainwright (D)
m.
Sarah Bates (D)

Peter Jr. (D)
m.
Abigail Jenkins (D)

Lou Lou (D)

Denton (D)

Martin

Elizabeth "Beth"

Archibald "Archy"
m.
Kate Greene (d)

Justin

Rose

Susan

Rain Dancer (D)

Hawk

D   Deceased
d   Divorced
m.   Married
---- Affair
———— Twins

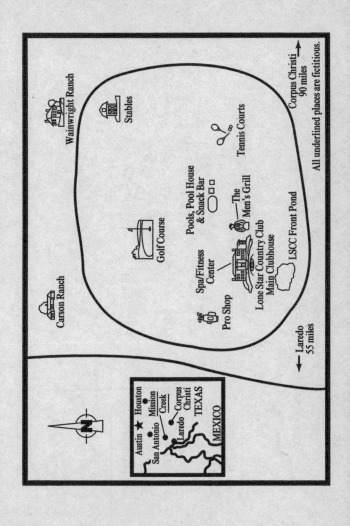

Wainwright Ranch

Stables

Tennis Courts

Carson Ranch

Golf Course

Pools, Pool House
& Snack Bar

The
Men's Grill

Spa/Fitness
Center

Pro Shop

Lone Star Country Club
Main Clubhouse

LSCC Front Pond

← Laredo
55 miles

Corpus Christi
90 miles →

All underlined places are fictitious.

N

Austin ★ Houston

Mission
Creek

San Antonio

Laredo

Corpus
Christi

TEXAS

MEXICO

One

Everything looked just the same, she thought.

Caitlyn Matthews stopped her car at Mission Creek Memorial Hospital and looked around. The automobiles and SUVs stacked side by side in the employees' parking area were the same ones that had been here last Tuesday. The American flag still snapped to attention with each hot gust of south-Texas wind. The original hospital building looked strong and impressive, but the windows of the new maternity wing looked a little shinier than the others. Maybe that was her imagination. If the wing already harbored nasty memories, then, Cait thought whimsically, it had the air of a haughty celebrity who was not about to reveal the skeletons in her closets.

She had worked at the hospital for the past four years now. The sight of it should have filled her with a sense of normalcy, of hope. Instead, she realized that it was entirely possible she was about to throw up.

She unclenched one hand from the steering wheel to press her fingers against her lips. *What's wrong with me? I can't be like this. It's just not acceptable.* Cait took her hand away from her mouth with a jerky motion and laughed aloud at the thought. A lot of things she would never have allowed before had been creeping into her life lately.

Her life was a shambles, a disaster. It was in sharp little shards at her feet, and she had no idea what to do about it. But she did know that having her life torn apart and tossed about for a few short days was not going to undo her permanently. She would just have to pick up the pieces and put them all back together again. What frightened her was that she was starting to think she might not be able to put them back in the same order they'd been in before.

"Give it time," Cait told herself. She had a plan. But first she had to force herself to simply step into the hospital again.

She got out of her dark-blue Ford compact and locked the door behind her, then jiggled the handle to make sure it was secure. She pivoted to the hospital and began to walk before she realized she'd better be absolutely positive her vehicle was locked. She went back and tested the handle again.

"Fine," she said. "It's fine." Of course it was. The car was locked up tight and in fine shape. In its two years she'd taken it in for service at three thousand, six thousand, twelve and eighteen thousand miles, almost right on the dot each time. It was steady, reliable.

She was the one falling off her rocker lately.

Cait turned away from the car like a marine drill sergeant. She made it through the front doors of the hospital just fine. But as it turned out, that was the easy part. The man she'd suddenly decided to give her virginity to after twenty-five otherwise chaste and uneventful years was right there in the lobby, staring at her.

It was unconventional, but Dr. Sam Walters prided himself on marching to a different drummer. He stepped off the elevator with a mission, towing the boy behind him by one hand.

Gilbert Travalini was nine years old, scared out of his mind and, in all likelihood, he was dying, though Sam had yet to give up the fight to turn that particular tide. New marrow would be transplanted into his bones at seven o'clock tomorrow morning. The match wasn't as close as Sam would have liked and there was a chance the boy's body would reject it, but until that happened, Gilbert was still a motor head and Sam happened to own one very fine, candy-apple-red Maserati. Said Maserati was currently parked outside.

"Let's go," he said, tugging the boy into the lobby. "If all that stuff about speed was just some macho bluff on your part, better cough up the truth now before you wet your pants."

"You're going to let me ride in it?" Gilbert's blue eyes bugged.

"I'm going to do better than that. I'm going to let you drive it."

The kid stumbled in thrilled shock. Sam caught his elbow and held him up. "Easy does it now."

"That's against the law," Gil said.

"Are you going to rat me out?"

"No! No, sir."

"Then come on. I've got thirty minutes before rounds and—"

And then she was there.

Sam's voice was chopped off in midsentence and he came to a stop. He had a single, inane thought: this isn't supposed to happen yet. They'd only gotten out of that underground room where they'd been held hostage a few days ago. He'd figured it would take Caitlyn Matthews weeks to recover and get back to work. At least, it would take the average woman that long.

But little Miss Tight Buns obviously considered it her patriotic, Hippocratic, fuss-budget duty to get back to work as soon as possible after the singularly worst event in her ultra-organized life, Sam thought. She'd probably do it if only to make *his* life miserable, he thought.

His eyes narrowed as she came toward him. A petite, waifish blonde, her every stride was measured and precise. That little chin of hers was held high, and her sapphire eyes moved neither left nor right. Every germ within a fifteen-yard radius either saluted or ran for cover at the sight of her, Sam decided sourly.

His heart, meanwhile, was pounding like a triphammer.

"What are you doing here?" he demanded when she came to a stop in front of him.

"I work here," Cait replied without looking at him. Then she leaned down to look into Gilbert's eyes. "Running off on me, are you?"

"No, ma'am. Yes, ma'am. I'll be back, though," the boy said, clearly rattled.

Cait straightened again and transferred her attention to Sam. "Where are you taking him, anyway?"

"Nowhere." Sam felt like a kid himself, one just caught in a naughty act by a particularly unpleasant teacher.

What was he supposed to do about this situation, anyway? He decided this was all her fault. No matter that he should have known it would eventually come to this when he'd first taken it into his head to touch her in that underground room. For that one insane, stress-induced moment he'd thought he would just taste her and that would be that. But he hadn't stopped there because something amazing and overwhelming about her had swum through him and over him and drove him to a place where nothing else mattered except the scent of her, the feel of her, her heat.

Now they were back at the hospital, back to being co-workers, and he couldn't seem to get his stride.

"Why are you guys in the lobby?" she asked in that quiet, even voice, bringing him back.

Sam looked around, then recovered enough to wink at Gil. "Could be just a wrong turn. Right, sport?"

"Knowing you, why do I doubt that?" Cait took Gil's other hand. "Come on, kiddo, back to bed with you."

"No! Please!" The boy pulled hard against her grip, forcing her to let go.

Cait looked at Sam again, frowning. "What are you up to?"

Sam felt temper slide into his blood. Maybe it mingled with his panic. "Tell you what. When I start reporting to my nurses, you'll be the first one I come to."

He saw her recoil. "I'm sorry," he said to her, then turned to Gil. "Go sit down over there for a minute." He pointed at the little lounge tucked in one corner of the lobby. The boy hurried off.

"That's the first sensible thing you've said yet," Cait commented.

"You just can't hold your tongue, can you?" That was a new side to the normally quiet Caitlyn, he thought, and it made something with hard, hot fists punch inside his brain. "You shouldn't be here. What's wrong with you, anyway? Why are you back at work so soon?"

"Why are you?"

"I'm a doctor. I have patients."

"So do I."

"Someone else can fill in for you. They've been doing it for days."

That chin of hers came up again. "Well, they don't have to do it any longer. The world didn't suddenly come to an end when we...when I...when Hines..."

He watched her come up against the issue of what had happened to them—between them—in that room and back off again. Okay, that was good. She was a complication his life didn't need. And there was no doubt he'd snag up *her* life pretty nastily, too. They were the two most disparate people you could ever imagine, and they still had to work together. They had to leave behind that underground room—and everything they had done there—and move forward.

His knees went a little weak as he considered the alternative—that she might think they shared some kind of...relationship now. He could always give her his ex-wife's phone number, he thought. Nancy could set her straight on that score.

He decided to avoid pursuing their current topic and switched gears. "I'm taking Gil for a ride," he said suddenly.

"In what?"

"My car."

"Why?"

"He's got this thing for *speed*mobiles. And he's dying."

He saw her wince, but then she rallied. "He can't possibly have been discharged. Do his parents know about this?"

"Are you questioning me again, Nurse?"

She backed off a step. "Of course not." Then something glinted in her eyes. That was new, too, he thought, startled. She'd always been docile to a fault.

"Yes," she amended.

"Well, don't. It's none of your concern."

"He's my patient. Have you considered the risk of infection if you take him out of here?"

He withered her with his gaze and glanced at his watch. "That's why he's chock-full of antibiotics. I'll see you for rounds in twenty minutes."

"Where can you take Gilbert Travalini in twenty minutes?" she persisted.

To the barren roads snaking through the federal land behind the Saddlebag bar, he thought, and to a brief, small slice of heaven before, God forbid, the boy actually saw the pearly gates for real. "Don't worry about it," he answered. "Get to work."

She backed off another step.

"Caitlyn—Nurse Matthews." He corrected himself fast. Her gaze lifted to his, a little too fast, a little too searchingly. Sam felt his stomach spasm. "It was a one-time thing. You know that, right?"

This time her expression didn't change. "Of course. I never intended for it to be anything else."

You were a virgin, damn it! The words blared through his head, though Sam held himself back from shouting them aloud. Virgins didn't run around suddenly unzipping their uniforms on a whim. Rigid, prissy little virgins didn't. *This* virgin shouldn't have. So why had she?

And why him?

"Please be careful," she said suddenly. She inclined her head toward the boy. "With whatever you're intending to do with Gilbert."

And that, he thought, was all the importance she gave to making love with the doctor she'd worked with and driven crazy for the past four years. Sam raked a hand through his dark hair. "Come on, Gilbert," he called. "Time to roll."

The boy launched out of his seat with more energy than he should have possessed. They headed for the lobby doors together. Sam didn't look back.

He didn't see her eyes fill with tears.

Cait completely forgot that she'd dreaded stepping foot back into this hospital. She blinked hard and fast against crying, and practically dove headfirst into the corridor that led to the new maternity wing. Everything inside her screamed to get away from Sam Walters before he saw her fall apart.

"Oh, God, what have I done to my life?" Suddenly Cait's starched spine crumbled and she leaned against the wall, hugging herself. She was shaking. Badly.

It was a one-time thing. You know that, right?

The truth was, she'd spent the past three days in a state of agonized expectancy because she hadn't actually been sure.

She hadn't seen him or heard from him since they'd been rescued from Branson Hines and the underground room where he'd held them hostage until Tabitha Monroe—the hospital administrator, who for some reason felt compelled to be Cait's friend when Cait very much preferred her solitude—had taken it into her head to have all twelve orange pounds of Cait's cat pose as a baby in a blanket in an effort to meet Hines's ransom demands. Cait scrubbed her hands over her face as she stepped into the maternity wing. Tabitha sometimes tended toward extremes, but it had worked. Sort of.

She veered left. The new wing was like no hospital she'd ever imagined working in. The walls were done in bright, primary colors that jarred her a little in her current mood. She passed the newborns in the nursery without looking at them. Her stride hitched up as she passed the storage room where Branson Hines had cornered twelve employees a week ago, changing her life forever.

She reached the nurses' station, then hesitated and looked around furtively.

No one was here. She'd banked on it. She knew hospital routine and right now, everyone would be gearing up for rounds, cleaning up after breakfast. She stepped behind the desk and found the large brown envelope she was looking for near the computer station. It was the one that would carry memos and other paperwork from this department to other areas of the hospital. She unwound the little string that held it closed, drove a hand into her pocket and came up with a slim, white envelope.

She'd printed Dr. Jared Cross's name in neat block letters across the front and underlined it three times. She'd sealed it with a little blob of white wax.

"Help me, please," she whispered, "before I lose my mind." She dropped her envelope into the bigger one, closed it again and fled the maternity wing.

She could have just gone to his office to ask for an appointment, sparing herself all this subterfuge. For that matter, she could have sent the note via the nurses' station in her own pediatrics unit. But she didn't want anyone to know what she was up to. She didn't want any of her co-workers to go stuffing their own mail inside the pediatrics envelope, recognizing her handwriting on a personal envelope to Dr. Cross.

They couldn't know. No one could know what was happening to her. And she certainly couldn't confide in a stranger, couldn't go outside the hospital to another psychiatrist. The mere thought nearly crippled her with panic. Maybe she wasn't his usual prepubescent patient, but Cait knew Jared Cross. He was the director of child psychiatry at Mission Creek Memorial, and something about him had always appealed to her. He was a little gruff, eminently practical, not given to maudlin emotion.

She would have to trust him with this. There was no one else.

Cait rode the elevator up to the pediatrics floor in the main building. She was in Chelsea Cambridge's room when Sam walked in. This time she was ready for him.

"Good morning, Doctor."

He scowled at her as he took the patient's chart from her hands. "So that's how we're going to play this, hmm?" he asked in an undertone.

Cait hesitated. It was as though they'd never spoken downstairs. Maybe he was going crazy, too. Or maybe she had imagined that whole encounter.

The very real possibility of that had her stomach rolling.

"It was a one-time thing," she said, just to be sure.

"That it was."

She turned away from him quickly to ease down the sheets on the little girl's bed because she wasn't at all sure what her expression would reveal at his response. Then she watched him gently palpate the child's abdomen, and her mind spun away.

Those hands...

Cait had a sudden, shattering image of them on her own skin, closing over her breasts, his breath hot where his face had been buried at her throat. She'd thought she'd been dying. Not because of anything Hines had done or might still do, but because for the first time in her life, she'd known what it was to be touched, really touched. And she had craved it, had needed it with something so strong it had vibrated inside her.

Why had she done it?

Because he'd been funny and kind and gallant in that room, neither outrageous nor as arrogant as she'd come to believe during the years she'd worked with him. Because she'd been terrified that God would give her no more days after that one, and because there was something huge in life she was going to miss if she didn't make love with that man right then, right there. Because he was devastatingly good-looking with those sometimes stormy, sometimes laughing eyes and the little cleft in his chin. For once in her life she'd wanted to do something wild and daring and exhilarating. She'd done it because she'd needed him.

"Nurse Matthews?"

Cait snapped back. "I'm sorry. What?"

"Would you like to pay attention here?"

"I was." Her breath still felt short. But he'd already looked away from her, toward the interns who had gathered behind them.

"Okay, guys, this is what you're *not* supposed to do when you're with a patient—phase out on something personal," he said to them.

Cait felt her face heat with embarrassment. "I didn't…"

He shot her a sardonic look, the kind that only he could muster. He went on with his examination of the child.

"Coming?" he asked her as the others began leaving the room.

Cait refused to meet his eyes. "I'll be right behind you."

"Make it snappy."

Out of nowhere, Cait felt anger bubble up in her. She gave him a sharp, little salute before she realized she was going to do it. She was fiercely glad when he looked startled.

They landed in Gilbert's room next. The boy was

back in bed, his color high. "Well," she said quietly, "he appears none the worse for wear."

"Questioning me again, Nurse?"

"Who, me? I wouldn't dream of it, my being your subordinate and all."

Satisfaction was something hot and sharp under the skin that wasn't entirely unpleasant, she discovered when he seemed unable to respond. She liked it.

He gave her his shoulder, picked up Gilbert's chart and addressed the interns again. That was when she saw Jared Cross hovering in the doorway. Cait stepped quickly aside when the psychiatrist motioned to her.

"You wanted to see me?" he asked.

She hadn't expected him to get her note so quickly, or to act on it so promptly. "Yes."

"I've got about twenty minutes until my first appointment. Do you have time now?"

Cait glanced back at Sam. He seemed oblivious to her now. She cleared her throat loudly, but he didn't glance her way.

To hell with him, then. "Okay," Cait said.

She matched Dr. Cross stride for stride down the corridor to his office at the end of the floor. To his credit, she thought he was mincing his steps a bit, allowing her to keep up. He was a good foot taller than her own five foot two. He was also a gentleman, of sorts. When they reached his door, he pushed it open and seemed to suggest she step through first when suddenly he made a move of his own. They hit shoulders in the threshold. Or at least, Cait thought, her shoulder nailed his upper arm.

"Sorry," she said quickly. Then, in his office, she

hesitated. "I, uh, wanted to see you in a professional capacity." She felt her face flame.

Dr. Cross went to his desk and sat, lacing his fingers together and catching them behind his head. Rumor had it that he had found himself a pretty heiress and was happily besotted these days. Cait thought it showed. He seemed more relaxed than she had ever seen him.

Maybe that was what happened to a person when sex turned out right, she thought.

"I gathered that," he answered. "Have a seat."

"I don't have a lot of time." But she took the chair across from him. She desperately needed his help, but now that she was here, she faltered. This sort of thing was never supposed to have happened to her. "I don't know where to start," she murmured.

Cross brought his hands down. "Want me to do it for you?"

She blinked at him. "How can you? You don't even know why I want to see you."

"Try this on for size. You're having a hell of a time getting back to the woman you were before the rest of Hines's hostages escaped through the vent in that storage room, before he returned in time to keep you and Sam Walters from doing the same thing."

"I...yes."

"Now, suddenly, you'll be going about your business and—wham!—blazing fury seems to come at you from out of nowhere."

Cait sat up straight. "You're good."

He grinned and she liked him better for it. "I memorize well and I read all the books."

"What books?"

"On post-traumatic stress disorder."

She sat up straighter. "I don't have a disorder."

"Tell me what's been happening to you lately."

With the simple question, she felt something begin to shake inside her. Cait sank back in her chair again. "It's not just Hines. He was crazy, a horrible person, but he's gone."

Cross nodded. "He's in jail. Which, theoretically, should make you feel safe again. But you don't."

Cait shuddered. "People like him don't happen to people like me, at least not twice in the same lifetime. And he's incarcerated."

"He was supposed to have been incarcerated once before."

It was true, Cait thought weakly. Hines had disrupted the ribbon-cutting ceremony for the new maternity wing, then tried to kidnap the son of Crystal Bennett, the hospital fund-raiser. Already wanted for other crimes, he'd been remanded to the maximum-security prison in Lubbock. Somewhere between Mission Creek and Lubbock he'd escaped to follow the hatred in his heart right back to the hospital. He'd uprooted her life, not to mention those of several other people. But she and Sam had been the only ones held hostage in a room beneath his house. And then—

No, she couldn't think of that again.

"Caitlyn?" Cross prodded.

She jumped. "I'm sorry. What?"

"You were saying?"

She felt herself flush. "I was about to say that I seem to be doing a lot of that lately—fading in and out. That's what I meant. Hines is over, behind me. But *I'm* different.''

"Flashbacks?" he asked. "Do you experience flashbacks to your time in that underground room?"

She felt Sam's hands on her breasts again. The heat that slid up over her skin, from her chest to her throat to her face, was excruciating. "Yes," she said quietly.

Cross was watching her closely, but he said nothing.

"I think the worst part is that I'm…I've become paranoid," she whispered, the final scalding admission. The word made her sound so…crazy.

"Checking your locks three, four, five times?"

"That's it." She swallowed dryly. "And I keep feeling like someone is…I don't know. Watching me. Following me."

Cross sat forward and put his elbows on his desk. "Describe your childhood to me in five easy sentences."

Cait's eyes went big. "What kind of a shrink are you? I thought that sort of thing was supposed to take weeks. 'Tell me about your parents.… Did you wet the bed?'"

He laughed. "I'm a shrink who has a few more minutes with you today and who wants you to schedule another appointment. But in the meantime I'd like to point something out to you, and I might be able to do it if you answer my question in a nutshell."

Cait took in air and shrugged. She felt fragile. "Okay. When I was two, my mother left me with her aunt so she could find a decent job in a larger city. She didn't come back."

"What about your father?"

Cait lifted one shoulder again carefully. "Who knows?"

"Where he was?"

"*Who* he was."

"Ah. Okay, what happened then?"

"My great-aunt died when I was four and from then until I was eighteen I pretty much bounced from foster home to foster home." She touched her hands to her cheeks. "I am so terribly embarrassed about the way I've been acting lately. Why does any of this matter?"

"I just wanted to nail down the fact that you had a shaky childhood."

"But it didn't affect me."

"Sure it did. Your childhood is directly responsible for the type of adult you've become. For every action, there's a reaction, and that goes for the human psyche, too. The reaction doesn't necessarily have to be negative. Maybe you never had a problem with your past before—until Branson Hines grabbed you."

Cait brought her chin up. "I put myself through college, then nursing school. I'm here. I did fine."

He nodded.

"Those foster parents were kind enough. No one was ever cruel to me!" She shouted it and was instantly mortified. "Oh, heavens."

"What?"

"*That.* That's what I mean! I'm volatile. I'm…I'm out of control."

Cross grinned. "I like that word. Control. Great nutshell word."

"Why?" she pleaded.

"Because that was what you've had your whole life—or at least from the time you left that last foster home and went to college. And now—" he snapped his fingers "—it's gone. Hines took from you something you've fought hard to never have to relinquish again."

"Control," Cait whispered.

Cross nodded. "Rumor has it that you run a pretty tight ship here at work. What about at home?"

She paid her rent months in advance just in case anything untoward should happen and she was suddenly unable to find the money. The apartment was hers, the first place she could really call home, and she would not lose it. "I…yes. I guess."

"You had no control over things when Hines took you," Cross went on. He laid his palms flat on the desk. "He proved that all your efforts in that area have been for naught. That could shake a person like you to the core. Anyway, here's the deal. You did the right thing in coming back to work today. But I'd recommend that you confront the site of your trauma, too, and all the people associated with it."

"The room where it started?" She didn't want to go there.

"And Sam Walters. Though you work with him, so I imagine you've already dealt with him, right?"

Sam. Cait bit her lip.

"Was that a problem?" Cross asked. "Seeing him again?"

"Of course not. I'll do whatever I have to do to get back to normal."

"Good." He watched her closely. "Caitlyn, is

there something else you want to tell me about your abduction?''

She jolted. "Like what?"

"I don't know. That's why I'm asking. You tell me. Something else that might have rocked your world during that time?''

She'd made love with Sam. "Absolutely not."

"People react in some startling ways when they think their time is running out."

"Not me."

"They do uncharacteristic things."

"I never got uncharacteristic until I got home again. *That's* when all this started."

Cross stood. "You'll tell me sooner or later. I do want you to make another appointment. It would probably work best if you came in on your day off. We'll have more time together that way."

Cait pushed to her feet, as well. "Okay." She was back to being polite and agreeable. For now, she thought a little wildly. Who knew how long it would last?

"I'm sorry this happened to you, to everyone Hines touched."

Cait nodded. "Thank you. But he's gone now."

"With my help, you'll get the old Caitlyn back. But I seriously doubt if she'll ever be quite the same person she was before all this happened."

Cait squeezed her eyes shut. She was so desperately afraid of that. "I've got to go."

She fled Cross's office without making a second appointment, but they both knew she would be back.

Hines can't take me away from me! she wanted to holler. And as for Sam...well, just as he had said, it was a one-time thing. Time would pass and what they had shared would fade from her memory. And that was best. It was why she had prayed since they'd been released from that room, that he *wouldn't* call her, wouldn't try to get in touch with her. She'd seen woman after woman hang with bated breath on a man's every whim and action and spoken word— every one of those things out of their control. She would *not* let that happen to her.

Cait turned into the nurses' station again and came nose to nose with Sam's angry face.

"Where the hell have you been?" he snarled.

Two

The world was clearly going to hell in a handbasket, Sam thought, watching Cait open and close her mouth in shock at his outburst.

One minute everything had been perfectly normal. He'd known himself inside and out. The world around him was just predictable enough to offer comfort without driving him crazy. Then Branson Hines had crashed into his life, showing him that he wasn't so much the hero, after all. And now that they were free of the man, this woman seemed to stubbornly resist going back to the way she was supposed to be, the way she'd always been before.

''Excuse me,'' she said, trying to step around the desk and pass him.

''The hell I will.'' He blocked her way. ''You owe me an explanation.''

''For what, pray tell?''

''Pray tell?'' Suddenly Sam grinned. That was the Caitlyn Matthews he'd always known. Then again, the old Nurse Matthews had never argued with him or contradicted him. And now, unless he missed his guess, she was actually questioning him about his annoyance.

His blood pressure spiked again. ''You walked out on me in the middle of rounds!''

"No, I did not."

"You were there, then you just wandered off."

"I attempted to tell you I was leaving. You wouldn't acknowledge me."

"Maybe you didn't try hard enough!"

"Would you kindly stop shouting? You're embarrassing me."

"I ought to write you up for this! To hell with your pride."

Then she shocked him. She placed both hands on his chest and shoved. "You're in my way."

"I'm—" He broke off, dumbfounded, his thoughts fragmenting. "You're out of your mind!"

She swiveled on one hip to glance back at him. "Could be. If I were you, I'd watch my step. There could be an ax murderer lurking inside me. You wouldn't want to tick her off." Then she walked away.

"You know, after everything that happened to us last week, I don't think that's very funny," he called after her.

Sam heard his own words and almost choked. He was the practical joker of the pediatrics floor, the one to whom not much was sacred, unless it affected a patient, the one who took a very sick boy speeding around federal land in a Maserati the day before surgery.

Caitlyn seemed to catch the incongruity of his statement, too. She stopped again. "I know what Hines took from me, Sam," she said, looking back. "What did he take from you?"

He refused to be sidetracked. "A nurse, for starters. What if I had needed you ten minutes ago?"

"As you pointed out earlier, there are plenty of others on the floor who can do my job. I'm non-essential."

"Damn it, I never said that." He'd always had a good rapport with the nursing staff. After all, most of them were women.

"You implied it, then."

"I was making the point that *I* had to come back to work. You didn't!"

"You're shouting again, Sam."

He was going to choke her.

Then it hit him. She'd never once called him by his first name until the time he'd buried himself inside her in that room. Even when Hines had been shuffling them along at gunpoint, she'd called him Dr. Walters. Now she'd said *Sam* twice in the last minute.

Things were getting way out of hand.

"Go back to work," he said shortly.

"I was trying to until you detained me." She set off down the corridor again, her tight little hips twitching. Had they ever twitched before? He couldn't be sure. He'd never quite gotten past her cool stuffiness until she'd whispered, "Show me how" in his ear.

So he had. He had shown her. And now he couldn't get her out of his mind.

"Doctor?" One of the other nurses approached him, frowning. "Are you all right?"

"Why wouldn't I be?" Stupid question, Sam thought. But Hines had derailed him a lot less than little Miss Fancy Hips, who'd just turned into a room down the corridor.

Sam brought his focus back to the nurse before him. Her name was Angelina Moffit. She was a brunette of staggeringly appealing proportions—the type he usually went for. He opened his mouth to tease her, then just waved a hand in abject disgust with himself. For the first time in his memory, words failed him. "Oh, to hell with it."

He left her and started down the hall. This, he thought, was going to end right here and now. He caught up with Jared Cross just as the psychiatrist was ushering a woman and her daughter into his office. "I need a minute with you," he said peremptorily.

Cross lofted a brow. "Most people make an appointment."

"I don't have time for that. This can't wait. It's important."

The psychiatrist watched him for a beat, then nodded. He stuck his head in his office and said a word to the woman, then he returned. "Five minutes."

"Fine." Sam turned to a door across the hall and threw it open. He stepped into his office after Cross and closed the door, being careful to turn the lock. "Have a seat." He said it like an order.

"That's usually my line." But Cross sat. "What's going on?"

Sam went behind his desk and sat, as well. There was no way to handle this, he thought, other than to dive right in. "I'm losing my mind."

Jared Cross laughed. "My practice is thriving. I ought to start charging more."

Sam scowled at him, not understanding. He raked his fingers through his hair, agitated.

Cross relaxed, leaning back to rest one ankle on his knee. "Okay. Tell me about your childhood."

Sam felt his eyes go to slits. "You're kidding, right?"

"No, not entirely. Cooperate with me."

"Well, I didn't wet the bed, that's for sure."

"You?" Cross shook his head. "No, I can't imagine that you did."

"What's that supposed to mean?"

"You've led a gilded life."

Sam thought about it and eased back in his own chair. "Yeah, right." He shrugged. "What's to tell? My parents have been married for almost forty-five years. I had dinner there last Sunday. The only thing they said to each other was 'Pass the salt,' in the exact same tones they used when I was six."

"Ah." Cross steepled his fingers under his chin. "School?"

"Straight A's, for the most part."

Cross grinned. "I've been your colleague for some time now and I know you're not *that* smart."

Sam relaxed enough to laugh a little. "I did a hell of a lot better with the female teachers, I can tell you that. Is this supposed to give me some insight as to what's wrong with me?"

"Yes. Because I'm smarter."

Sam laughed outright. Then Jared got serious.

"Try this on for size. My guess—knowing you as long as I have—is that you learned early on that what you failed to accomplish with your brain, you could always wing on your charm."

Sam didn't like the sound of that, but he nodded cautiously. "That's me. Charming."

"Personally, I think you rely too much on the knowledge that your looks and your talents of persuasion can get you out of pretty much any sticky situation."

"People *pay* you for this?"

"You'll have my bill in the morning. In the meantime, let's get back to what I was saying. When you were abducted last week, you ran headfirst into a brick wall. For the first time in your life, you hit up against something you couldn't finesse your way out of."

"Correction. I *did* get us out of it."

Cross waited.

"Okay, with some help." And, Sam thought, things had been looking pretty dismal until Tabitha Monroe and Jake White had arrived. Yeah, that bothered him.

"Now you find yourself doubting your every move in areas that had always been your strong suits," Cross continued.

"Not every move." Though he'd had a horrible moment in surgery yesterday, Sam thought. What was the sense in denying it? *He* had asked this guy for help. "Just most of them."

"It's called post-traumatic stress disorder," Cross said.

Sam stiffened. "I don't do stress and I don't do disorders."

"You do now."

"That's bull—"

Cross held up a hand to cut him off. "It basically happens when the predictable order of one's life is suddenly derailed by any sort of catastrophic event.

Things you once put trust in are no longer viable. You find yourself reacting differently, in ways you never considered before.''

Sam breathed again. There it was. The answer. *That* was why he couldn't get little Nurse Sweetness off his mind. ''So give me something for it.''

Cross shook his head. ''No can do.''

''Come on, there's a drug for everything these days. Turn me into me again.''

''You're a doctor, a surgeon. Kids' lives depend on you. I'm not prescribing you so much as an aspirin. Besides, it wouldn't work, anyway.''

There was that, Sam thought, feeling chastened. But he was desperate. ''What, then?''

''I want to see you again. Make an appointment this time. We'll talk our way through it.''

''I'm not going to start seeing a shrink over this.''

''You already have.''

Sam rubbed his jaw. ''I'll think about it.''

Cross stood. ''In the meantime, you might want to think about confronting the source of your trauma.''

''Come on, Jared, 'trauma' is a little harsh.''

''The scene of the crime, then.''

Sam's mind flashed immediately to Caitlyn—and what they had done in that basement room. ''You can't be serious.''

Cross gave him an odd look and nodded. ''Try visiting the place where it began, where you started realizing you were a day late and a dollar short on saving yourself and Nurse Matthews.''

''The storage room.'' Sam breathed again. That he could do. ''Why not? It beats the hell out of tangling with little Nurse Prim-and-proper.''

"You seem more focused on your hostage situation than on the actual abduction," Cross observed. "What exactly happened to the two of you in that underground room, anyway?"

I lost my mind for a woman I never thought I liked, Sam thought, and now she's metamorphosed on me. "Nothing."

Cross shrugged. "You'll tell me. Sooner or later."

Sam had a staggering thought. "This post-traumatic stress disorder could have happened to Cait, too, right?"

"Cait?"

"Caitlyn. Nurse Matthews."

Cross fought a grin. "Presumably. If the normal order of her world was rocked."

"This sort of thing could really change people," Sam mused.

"It changed you."

"It's tripped me up a little, that's all."

"You know, after we're finished with the stress disorder, we can work on your ego problem if you like."

Sam made a gesture in Cross's direction to tell him what he thought of that. Then he got to his feet, too. "You've already fixed me. Thanks for taking the time."

"Make an appointment, anyway."

Sam watched Cross leave the office and he took a deep, steadying breath. It wasn't him. Well, not entirely. It was Caitlyn, too. She'd gone wacky on him. *He* was essentially fine.

He had pre-op routines to do on Gilbert. Sam headed for the door. He stepped into the corridor almost squarely into Dr. Kimberlie Leon's impressive chest.

"Hey there," he said, grinning. "Looking for someone?"

"As a matter of fact, I am. You." She tossed back her mane of long, dark-blond hair. She was the newest addition to Mission Creek Memorial's staff—an oncology physician.

"My lucky day." He leaned a shoulder against his door. "What can I do for you?" He was back, Sam thought. Oh, yeah, he was definitely back on his stride.

Then he looked over the doctor's shoulder. He saw Cait Matthews coming toward them down the corridor, shoulder to shoulder with one of the interns, a dark-eyed Lothario from somewhere out West. California, Sam thought it was. As he watched, she tucked that tidy, short blond hair behind one of her ears and glanced up at the guy out of the corner of her eye. Then she laughed.

She'd been a *virgin* until a few days ago! Was she trying to turn that one inaugural event into a whole four-year term or something?

"Got to go," he said suddenly to Kimberlie.

"But—"

"Catch up with me later."

He left the doctor gaping after him and stepped back into his office. He slammed the door hard.

It was well after four before Cait returned to the maternity wing. She was so tired her legs felt weak.

She had managed to keep her contact with Sam to a minimum through the rest of the day, but each iso-

lated encounter with him had drained more out of
her. Emotions had been ricocheting through her for
the past eight hours—ups, downs, highs, lows and
everything in between. She'd found herself sneaking
peeks at him, remembering. Again. Then she'd found
herself hating him for his newfound brusqueness,
though she'd noticed that he was foul with everyone,
not just with her.

Maybe he, too, was having trouble regaining his
equilibrium after what had happened to them, she
thought as she made her way down the flamboyant
corridor. The absurdity of such an idea would have
made her laugh if she'd had the energy. The unflap-
pable, outrageous Sam Walters? Hardly.

Cait's feet stalled as she reached the storage room
across from the nursery. She touched the doorknob
tentatively, praying it would be locked and she could
just turn away from here and go home. Why did Jared
Cross want her to do this, anyway? Her every incli-
nation was to turn her back on what had happened,
to walk away from it, close it out, forget it. Then
again, if she'd been able to do that, she wouldn't
have gone to see him in the first place.

The door wasn't locked. Cait leaned into it and it
opened. She stepped over the threshold and let the
door swish shut behind her.

She took a few militant steps into the room, then
stood in the center of it with her arms crossed over
her breasts. Her heart started beating a little too
quickly. She unfolded her arms to press the heel of
her right hand to her chest. "This is ridiculous."

Her gaze slid over the shelves stacked with cardboard boxes. Someone had picked them up, she

thought, because they'd gone flying when Sam had briefly struggled with Hines the day the man had taken them. Hines had come back into the room to find the others escaping through the vent, and Sam had held him back long enough to keep him from grabbing the last woman in the duct. By then, of course, it had been too late for Sam and her.

Cait shivered and glanced at the hard plastic-and-metal chairs tangled together like some kind of absurd jungle gym in one corner. Then her eyes were drawn to the door, and the memories came rushing back....

"Let's go, let's go!" Hines shouted, waving his gun.

Cait took a step that way, then balked. The thought of leaving the room with him had cold sweat beading along her spine, between her breasts, under her arms. Then Dr. Walters was behind her and she couldn't back up anymore, couldn't get away.

"Do it. Just go ahead," he whispered. "I'm right behind you. We need to placate him until I have time to think our way out of this. I won't let anything happen to you."

She'd believed him, Cait realized, had trusted him blindly. Probably because, for the first time in her life, she hadn't been able to think her own way out of what was happening to her. Hines had forced them down the hall to a maintenance room and into a laundry chute there.

Now she went to the vent and placed her palm against the cool metal. Then she eased down to sit on the floor, pulling her knees up to her chest. She wasn't sure what was supposed to happen here. Was she supposed to feel miraculously better for confronting this place? Well, she didn't. She covered her face with her hands and closed her eyes.

Then she heard the door open.

For a single moment her heart seized. She was afraid to look to see who it was. She was suddenly, insanely sure that Hines was back to try again. He'd escaped. It was going to start all over again—except this time she was alone.

She kept her face covered, afraid to breathe. Then she recognized the tread of rubber-soled shoes on the linoleum. Hospital shoes. She pulled her hands away and opened her eyes. What she saw was very nearly worse than her imaginings.

Sam.

He didn't notice her in the shadows. He made a guttural sound of anger in his throat and walked over to the air-conditioning vent, punching his fist into it hard. The metal rang. Cait let out a yelp. He jerked around and spotted her.

"What are you doing here?" he demanded.

She'd die before she admitted she'd seen Jared Cross and he'd recommended it. "I could ask you the same question."

"I asked you first."

They both seemed to realize how juvenile that sounded. Sam looked away, and for a moment she thought he looked almost embarrassed. Then he went to the pile of boxes and began moving the ones on top. "I was looking for something."

Cait astounded herself by snorting. "And then the vent did something to offend you?"

He stopped moving and looked at her as though

she had changed color. "Damn it, would you stop doing that?"

"What?"

"Being sarcastic. It doesn't suit you."

"I don't know about that. I never really tried it on before."

"Well, you have now, and I don't like it. So knock it off."

"Correct me if I'm wrong, but I only report to you between the hours of eight and four. And that's on a *bad* day. If I want to be sarcastic on my own time, that's my choice."

His eyes—they were the color of chocolate in the dim light, she thought—almost bugged. "You just did it again!"

Suddenly the fight went out of her. Cait slumped back against the wall and looked away. "Please. Just leave me alone."

He was silent for a long time. "You're not doing okay with any of this, are you?" he asked finally.

His voice was kind. She brought her chin up quickly and looked at him once more. "I'm doing great. You?"

"Terrific. Good. No problem."

"Which explains perfectly why we're both here."

"I was looking for something," he said again.

"Then get it and go. Don't let me keep you."

He sat on the floor across from her, instead. "You know what part I liked the most?"

She knew, somehow, that he was talking about the ideas for escape they'd bounced back and forth during their first few hours in their underground prison.

What did it mean, that she was suddenly able to read his mind? "Which?"

"When you were going to hide in the ceiling pipes and drop down on him after I called him into the basement."

Cait sniffed. That one had been her idea. "You wouldn't have fit up there."

"You're too small to have done any damage to him. He would have thought a flea had landed on his back."

She felt anger kick in her again. "So you said at the time. But I believe you called me a sparrow."

"Flea, sparrow, same thing."

"Tell that to the itchy sparrow."

He stared at her again, then he laughed and shook his head. "You really have gone off your rocker."

Cait stiffened. "I'm not the one going around beating up ducts."

He ignored that. "I would liked to have seen it, though—you falling through the air like Wonder Woman."

Suddenly she felt hot again. Her skin felt excruciatingly warm, all her senses heightened. "I believe she was a bit more substantial than I am."

"'I believe,'" he mimicked. "That's good. You're sounding like you again."

"I was an English major before I decided to go into nursing," she said tightly.

"Why'd you change?"

"Nursing pays moderately better than teaching. Then again, teaching doesn't demand interaction with arrogant God's-gift-to-women doctors."

He looked genuinely affronted. "I'm not arrogant."

"You're arrogant."

"How am I arrogant?"

Cait pushed to her feet. She crossed to the door, but she wasn't leaving. She stopped there and rested one shoulder against the frame, a wide, cocky grin on her face. "'Looking for someone?'" she mimicked him.

He watched her, mystified.

She left the door and turned around to face it. She put a simpering look on her face and tossed back an imaginary mane of hair. "'As a matter of fact, I am. You,'" she said in a falsetto.

When she turned around this time, she saw the light dawn in his eyes.

"Kimberlie Leon?" he asked. "You were too far away to hear what I said to her."

"Obviously, not far enough." Cait leaned back against the wall.

"Regardless. That wasn't arrogance."

"Okay. Cockiness, then."

"I was flirting."

"Well, if the way you slammed your office door was any indication, your technique needs work." She came back at him quickly, because she hated the hot shaft of something unseen and inexplicable that hit her in the gut, something bizarrely like jealousy. "She was all over Kenny Estrada the moment you were gone," she added.

"The intern?" Sam scowled. "She was?"

"She was."

"I guess that took *you* down a peg." He shot at her.

It had, actually. "Why would it?"

"*You* were flirting with *him*."

She crossed her arms. "I don't flirt."

"Maybe not two weeks ago, but you were sure as hell doing it today."

"No, I wasn't."

He got to his feet and proceeded to pick his steps across the room. He looked coyly out of the corner of his eye and gave a high-pitched little giggle as he tucked invisible hair behind his ear. "That's flirting."

Cait opened her mouth in outrage. Then a laugh came up from her belly. She clapped a hand over her mouth in an unsuccessful effort to stifle it, and then a sobering thought hit her. This was just the way he had been in that underground room. Whenever she'd started to come undone, he'd made her laugh until her panic had subsided.

Cait dropped her hand and turned around again to reach for the door handle. "I'm leaving."

"By the way, you're not less substantial than Wonder Woman," he said suddenly, stopping her. "Not in all areas."

She whirled back to him. Her heart kicked her chest and vaulted into her throat. "What?"

"I guess I would know." His gaze fell to her breasts.

Heat poured through her, almost making her knees buckle. Why was he talking about that? "Don't talk about that. It was a one-time thing."

"Yeah, it was. But I was just making an observation."

"Well, don't."

"You're blushing," he said.

"I don't blush, either."

"Right, and you don't cut men off at the knees."

"What? I never did that!"

He needed to talk about this, Sam realized. Coming back to this room sure as hell wasn't doing it for either of them. She was still just as unpredictable as she'd been all day. So he needed to put what had happened between them right out there in the air and toss it around a little, he decided. *Then* he could forget about it.

"Show me how," he whispered.

"Show you what?" Sam noticed that her voice went thin. It was almost a squeak.

"That's what you said to me when I kissed you." He watched more color fly into her face. "Face it, lady, you were the instigator in all that."

"That's preposterous!" Now her eyes were shooting fire. "*You* kissed *me!* It was the farthest thing from my mind! We were sitting there sharing that bag of peanuts you found in your pocket, then you started feeding them to me and then you just…you just…kissed me!"

That was exactly how it had happened, Sam thought, so he wouldn't win any points trying to argue it. He tried another tack. "And you needed me to tell you how to kiss? Was that why you said, 'show me how'?"

"No!"

"Then the rational deduction is that you were not talking about kissing when you said those words."

"I don't even remember saying them!"

"Oh, honey, you said them. Trust me on that one."

"Well, then, I was…I was…"

Sam waited.

"Go to hell!" she shouted.

He threw back his dark head and laughed. "I was waiting for you to say something like 'You, sir, are no gentleman.'"

She sniffed. "Except we always knew that."

Sam found himself closing the distance between them. "Four years, and I never knew you had such a tongue on you, Nurse Matthews."

She backed up against the door. "You've seen the last of my tongue."

"Have I?"

"What's gotten into you? It was a one-time thing!"

"So was the burning bush, but people are still talking about it."

"I don't want to talk!"

"That's a change, then. You did it nonstop the whole time we were in that room. The only thing you didn't tell me was at what age you were potty-trained."

She pressed her hands to her cheeks. "There was nothing else to do but talk."

"Oh, we thought of something."

She moved her hands to clap one against her tummy. "Stop this."

Okay, he thought, relaxing for the first time all day.

He knew a rattled woman when he saw one. She wasn't as indifferent to that whole business between them as she pretended to be. His ego was assuaged.

Now, he thought, he could put it behind him.

He took another step toward the door and she jumped back again, hitting it so hard the collision hurt *him.* His first instinct was to ask if she was all right. He touched a finger to the underside of her chin, instead. "Relax."

She smacked his hand away. "Don't touch me!"

He backed up gladly. Her skin was too soft. "Are you going to stand there all night, or are you going to move so I can leave and go home?"

Cait jerked aside so he could get to the door. "Be my guest."

He opened it and stepped through.

"You said I was rigid, too," she said suddenly. "You didn't just call me a sparrow. You said I was *rigid.*"

He looked back at her. The conversation was supposed to be finished. He'd done what he'd meant to do. He'd gotten her out of his blood. But now something in his gut hitched all over again.

"You *were* rigid," he said, "right up until you started taunting Hines like some kind of madwoman." And that had blown his mind away.

She gave a quick little nod. "Okay, then. I just wanted to get that straight for the record."

"Consider it straight. You have unplumbed depths, Nurse. Duly noted." Damn it! She looked bewildered and pleased by the compliment, and he felt something go hinky in him again. He felt himself wanting to kiss her one more time.

"Let's go," he said quickly. "Are you done communing with the laundry chute?"

She stepped through the door after him and shut it smartly behind her. "In my own fashion. I might mention that at least I didn't destroy my knuckles in the process."

Sam looked down at his right hand. She was right. He was bleeding. He felt marginally like an idiot until they took four or five strides down the hall. Then he was distracted by the nervous shift of her shoulders. She hesitated and looked back the way they'd come.

"What?" he asked.

She shook her head. "Nothing."

He walked with her to the employees' parking area. He wasn't surprised when she stopped beside a car that was small, practical and ugly. It was exactly what he would have expected her to drive—a week ago. That comforted him a little until he got to his Maserati and looked back.

Then he watched her through her windshield. She started playing with that damned zipper again, the one on the front of her scrubs top. She tugged it down a little. He got a peek of skin—he knew it was as smooth and pale as alabaster—then she fanned herself from the heat with her hand. She reached to the passenger seat and a second later she pushed dark, wraparound sunglasses onto her face. When she turned out of the lot, the wind tickled her hair through the open windows.

It was over, damn it. Over. A one-time thing. But suddenly Sam had to inhale hard just to breathe.

The woman tailed them as far as the lobby, her anger pushing hot and steady at the inside of her skull.

It had been a bit of luck, finding them together. Otherwise, she would never have known that they were still cozy. Up until now, she'd just been keeping an eye on *him*. He was her answer, her way out, the clever doctor who collected women like trophies, then tossed them aside.

He was the one who would give her everything she'd ever wanted. Except now…now he'd come out of that storage room with the breathless little blonde. It was a wrinkle and it infuriated the woman. It caught her off guard and was going to force her to adjust her plans.

She waited until they turned out of the corridor, then she hurried after them. She'd had a bad moment when the bitch looked back over her shoulder as though knowing she was being watched, and that made her more cautious. She finally landed in the lobby at the same time they pushed through the outside doors.

She hurried to the glass and watched him standing there, staring after the sweet, wimpy nurse.

She'd have to fix this, she thought. This time she wasn't going to lose.

Three

Normally Cait used the drive home from work to plan the evening ahead. She considered which chores she could do to free up time on her days off for more pleasurable pursuits, like scouting out a flea market. She thought about what new book she might start reading and letters she really ought to write.

But tonight, as she pulled out of the hospital parking lot, she decided that what she really wanted most in life was a glass of wine.

What had that been back there with Sam? Her heart had stopped gallivanting, but still thudded in a strange way. The pit of her stomach still felt ticklish. He'd been teasing her, she thought, and he had mentioned *it*. Not once, not twice, but repeatedly.

Yes, she decided, she definitely wanted a glass of wine. It would be very soothing. She pulled over to the curb for a moment because she wasn't quite sure how to go about such a thing. Stop at a bar? She'd noticed the Saddlebag at the edge of town a time or two, and there was always the Lone Star Country Club. But truth be told, her insides went a little squirmy at the idea of sashaying into such an establishment by herself. Okay, she thought, she'd find a liquor store.

She pulled away from the curb and spotted one a

few minutes later. It occurred to her that she'd passed it every morning and night on her way to and from the hospital without ever really noticing it. Of course, she felt very strongly about keeping her eyes on the road while she was driving. A fender bender would really disrupt her life. But these days such a calamity seemed like...well, less of a calamity.

"Being taken hostage with God's gift to women is infinitely worse," she muttered, and pulled her little car up to the curb one more time.

She got out and locked the door. She was halfway across the sidewalk when it happened again, that itchy feeling at the back of her neck, the humming urgency inside her to make sure the car was absolutely secure. Cait stalled and rubbed a hand over her nape.

"No," she said. She wasn't going to do this anymore. She was going to get better.

"I didn't even ask you yet," said a man approaching up the pavement.

Cait turned her head, then literally gaped at him. He was one of the best-looking men she'd ever seen, right up there with Sam Walters. Why had she never noticed before how many truly handsome men there were running around Mission Creek?

"I beg your pardon?" she asked uncertainly.

"You said no."

She laughed a little breathlessly as she understood. "I did that, yes."

He grinned. "One of my best friend's wives talks to herself a lot, too. They haven't slapped her into the nuthouse yet."

Cait nodded. "I just started doing it recently," she admitted.

He threw back his dark head and laughed. "Points for honesty," he said. "I like that. I'm Ricky Mercado, by the way."

"Oh! I've heard of you."

"Good or bad?"

"Bad, actually." Had she really just said that?

He didn't seem offended. "Well, I've reformed."

"How much?" Cait almost choked on her tongue. Was she flirting again? Such a thing could only get her into hot water, especially with this man. She had to knock it off right now.

"Listen," he said, motioning at the store, "if you were heading in there for something to drink, why don't I spare you the trouble? I'd really like to take you out for a cocktail."

Cait felt the sidewalk shift beneath her feet. He wanted to take her out? Just like that? "Thank you, no."

"You're sure?"

"I've got plans," she lied, and was shocked at the ease with which the words rolled off her tongue.

"Too bad."

He looked as if he meant it, she thought bemusedly. She took another step toward the liquor store. A man like Ricky Mercado would gobble her up whole. There was something dangerous about him, some mob connection if she remembered correctly, not to mention his very air. Then again, the mob in Mission Creek had been more or less dismantled over the summer.

Was she actually thinking about accepting his offer? Cait fled into the store before her tongue could betray her again.

After twenty minutes she finally made her choices—a cabernet and something intriguingly called cactus schnapps.

The cost exceeded the cash she had in her purse, as it was right before payday, so she had to use a credit card. Normally she only used credit cards for emergencies. She almost changed her mind, but the clerk was looking at her impatiently. Vowing to write a check for the balance that very night, before they could charge her interest, she handed over the plastic.

She'd never be able to buy her own home if she tossed money away on such things as interest payments on credit cards, she thought. Then she had the sudden realization that it hadn't seemed very important when she'd been coming undone in Sam Walters's arms.

"Stop!" she told herself. She had to stop dwelling on him! Cait pressed her hands to her cheeks.

The clerk stopped moving just as he was about to run the card through a little machine. "You don't want to buy it, after all?"

"Of course I do." Cait waved a hand impatiently. "Just finish there."

Three minutes later she hurried back to her car with her purchases. When she got home, her landlady was pouring water on the flowers lining the walkway of the pretty white house on the street. Cait lived above the garage in the back. After she tucked her car into one of the spaces, she came out to find the elderly woman waving to her.

"Hello, Mrs. Brody!" she called back.

"What have you got there?" The old woman motioned to the bag in Cait's arms.

"This?" Cait looked down at the bag. "I thought I'd have a glass of wine with supper." She decided not to mention the cactus concoction.

She looked up in time to see the woman frown. Cait remembered too late that Mrs. Brody was a teetotaler.

"It's been a particularly difficult week," Cait added.

The woman's expression softened. "Poor dear. What all happened to you in that man's basement, anyway?"

"Nothing!"

The woman looked flabbergasted at the outburst. Cait turned tail and jogged to the steps at the side of the garage that led up to the second floor. She ran up them and closed the door hard and securely behind her.

The best thing she could do with herself now was prepare supper, she decided, and sip some wine while she cooked. She set the bag on her kitchen counter and hurried to the bedroom to change out of her scrubs.

It was a room she'd always cherished. There was a blue-and-white Amish wedding-ring quilt on the single bed. The furniture was pine and somewhat plain, but she'd added blue Cape Cod curtains to the single window and had warmed things up with a cheval mirror in one corner and a quaint antique washstand in the other. There were a few blue-silk flower arrangements, as well, and a solitary framed photo on the dresser of the mother she couldn't remember.

Cait stripped out of her scrubs and shoved everything into the hamper just inside her closet door. A knock sounded at the front door at the same time.

Several months ago, such an event would have been preposterous—she never had visitors. But lately Tabitha Monroe had taken to stopping by without warning. Or it could be Mrs. Brody, she thought, to pass further opinion on her bottle of wine. It could even be Sam.

Her heart stalled.

Given their conversation this afternoon, she was no longer even remotely sure what he was capable of. Cait rushed to the dresser and dragged out a pair of shorts, hopping into them on her way to the closet. She snagged a short-sleeved blouse off a hanger and buttoned it with fumbling fingers as she headed back to the living room. She was about to pull open the door when everything inside her froze.

It could be Sam...or it could be Branson Hines. Or some other raving lunatic determined to unravel her life. "Hines is in jail," she whispered resolutely. "And it can't happen to the same woman twice in one lifetime." Then again, why couldn't it? Where was that written?

"Cait?" Tabitha's voice came through the door. "I know you're in there. Mrs. Brody said you just got home."

Cait breathed again and threw the locks. She'd had two more installed yesterday, and though she didn't remember doing it, she had obviously engaged all three when she'd come in a little while ago. "Hi," she said.

The breeze plucked at Tabitha's dark-blond curls. She held a large brown bag and she shoved it toward her. "I brought Chinese."

Cait took the bag because she knew Tabitha would let go of it one way or the other. The hospital administrator was trying hard to improve on her workaholic tendencies, but she still had a waste-no-time edge to her. "I don't like Chinese," Cait protested.

"Everybody likes Chinese," Tabitha scoffed. "Can I come in?"

Cait also knew from past experience that it would do no good to say no. And she actually liked Tabitha. Her friendly persistence just made her nervous. "Sure." She stepped back from the door.

Tabitha swept inside. "I didn't think you needed to be cooking on your first day back to work," she said by way of explanation.

"I find cooking therapeutic." But Cait carried the bag into the kitchen and peered into it before she set it down and returned to the living room. "There's enough in there for five people!"

"Two," Tabitha corrected. "I'm joining you. I've already been to visit Jake. I'll go back to the hospital after we eat."

At the mention of Jake White, Cait recalled that the cop had actually proposed to Tabitha. It left Cait with a vague, wistful feeling.

"How's he feeling?" she asked. Jake had been shot rescuing Sam and her from Hines.

"He's chipper. Eager to go home. How's Billy?"

On cue, the cat belly-wormed his way out from

beneath Cait's dark-red Western-style sofa. "Not so chipper," she said. "I think you cost him one of his lives." Disputing that, the cat yawned and began cleaning himself as though he hadn't a care in the world.

"How was I supposed to know he was going to freak out like that and nearly botch the rescue?" Tabitha went and gathered up the cat, crooning to him.

"Cats hate loud noises. Gunshots especially. Hostage scenes are not their favorite things."

"Poor baby." Tabitha stroked him, then she put him down again abruptly. "Okay, break out the Mandarin beef."

Cait wrinkled her nose.

"It's for me. I brought you almond chicken. That can't bother your sensibilities too much."

Cait nodded. She never ate red meat. It just seemed so…barbaric.

Tabitha had already invaded the kitchen. Cait followed her in time to see her open the bag from the liquor store. "Hey, what's this?"

Cait flushed. "I sort of got a wild hair on my way home from work."

"*You* did?"

Cait pulled her spine straight. "I have unplumbed depths."

"Who told you that?"

"Sam Walters."

Tabitha's brows climbed her forehead. "Tell me all about *that*."

Cait felt treacherous heat trying to steal over her again. "There's nothing to tell."

"Hmm. Well, apparently he got to know you a whole lot better in three days than I have in months."

"He didn't get to know me."

"Then explain this business about depths." But Tabitha didn't wait for an answer. She began pulling cartons out of her own bag, then helped herself to the cupboard and got plates. "Where are your wineglasses?"

"Um, I don't have any." Cait hurried to another cupboard and found two jelly glasses. Buy a jar of jelly and get a glass you could use forever, to boot. Who could argue with that?

Tabitha tucked her chin as she considered them, then finally shrugged in acceptance. She plucked the cabernet out of its bag. "What are the odds that you actually own a corkscrew?"

"Excellent." Cait pulled one, still wrapped in plastic and cardboard, from a drawer. Then she shrugged sheepishly. "It just seemed like one of those things everyone should own. It was on sale."

Tabitha took it and attacked the bottle. Five minutes later, they were seated and dishing up Chinese food. Cait discovered the almond chicken wasn't half-bad.

"There was one home I was in—I think I was about eight—where the husband worked nights and the woman was always shoveling takeout at us kids," she explained. "I think that's where I learned an aversion to Chinese food."

Tabitha's fork stalled on its way to her mouth. "Takeout is relatively expensive."

"That particular family had a lot of state kids."

And they received a stipend from the government for every one of them, Cait thought.

"You never talk much about your childhood," Tabitha said.

Cait got up for more wine. "I'm sorry."

"For what?"

"For boring you." She poured, topping off both glasses without thought.

"You're not. I've always wondered what makes you so straitlaced."

"I have unplumbed depths!" Cait burst out. Then she flushed.

Tabitha's brows lifted again. "Sorry. I forgot that part." She chomped down onto an egg roll. "You've been through a lot lately. What happened in that underground room, anyway? You never did tell me."

Cait felt her skin turn to glass. "Nothing."

"You spent seventy-two hours in there."

"Hines was in and out. He didn't stay, but we could hear him walking around in the house upstairs whenever he was around."

Tabitha waited. "And?" she prompted when Cait said nothing more.

Cait kept chewing, focusing hard on her food. But Tabitha remained quiet, waiting, not willing to change the subject.

Cait sighed and put her fork down. "He already had bottled water and crackers down there in the basement. I told Jake that. Jake said that was because Hines had planned the whole thing." Tabitha's Jake had been the detective assigned to the hostage situation. "So we ate and we tried to figure out ways to get free. But the basement door was locked from the outside and the windows were so tiny not even I could fit through one. We tried banging on them for a while, but they faced the backyard and no one heard us.''

''What did you talk about?''

Everything but how old she was when she was potty-trained, Cait thought. She sipped wine, then suddenly found it hard to swallow. ''Mostly about me. I think I was nervous. I must have talked a lot.''

Tabitha nodded. ''That makes sense.''

''And he called me a sparrow. A rigid sparrow. I just felt like I had to defend myself against that.'' So she'd given him her whole life story.

''You told him about the foster homes?'' Tabitha looked surprised.

Cait shrugged. ''No one was ever unkind to me in any of them.''

''What else?'' Tabitha asked. ''What else did you two talk about?''

''I don't know!'' Cait cried. ''Missed chances. Lost dreams. Plans for the future. What do two people talk about when they're stuck in a room together for hours and hours on end?''

''Talk wouldn't have been high on my list of guesses in the first place,'' Tabitha said dryly. ''That's not Sam Walters's rep with a good-looking woman.''

''Nothing happened!'' Cait shouted. Then she went still, frowning. ''Good-looking? I'm not good-looking.''

''You're cute as a button and haughty to boot. Get off it.''

''Haughty?''

Tabitha nodded. "With that don't-touch-me air you've got going on."

"How can you say that?"

"I just think it would be a real challenge for a Sam Walters-type to see if he could touch you."

The hurt that raced through her almost stole Cait's breath. It was very cold and seemed to numb her nerve endings. Was that all she had been? A challenge?

Of course, she thought. It was the only thing that made sense. He'd gone out of his way this morning to make sure she knew it had been a one-time thing. Why, then, had she believed that it'd had something to do with getting to know her?

"Well, he didn't," she said tightly. She stood quickly to take her plate to the sink.

"I'll pass the word, then."

Cait whipped back to face her. "Why?"

"Because everyone in the hospital is wondering and it will kill the rumors. Come on, Cait. Pretty nurse. Knockout womanizing doctor. One basement room. Three days. What would *you* think?"

"I wouldn't think about it at all! It would be none of my business!"

"Unfortunately the rest of the hospital staff doesn't share your high ideals." Tabitha stood, as well, and began cleaning up the takeout packages.

Cait hugged herself, distraught. Now she was another Sam Walters statistic!

Tabitha glanced her way and her expression softened. She dropped a hand on Cait's shoulder in comfort. Cait twitched. She wasn't used to being touched. Tabitha took her hand away.

"It'll all blow over as soon as Sam sets his sights on something else in a skirt," she assured her. "That's the way gossip mills run. Anyway, I've got to go. I told Jake I'd be back in an hour."

"Of course. Thanks for stopping by." Cait realized that this time, for the first time, she genuinely meant it.

They were halfway back to the door when Tabitha turned around. "I almost forgot. I'm supposed to pester you about coming to the hospital's End of Summer Ball next weekend."

Cait frowned. "Who told you to pester me?"

"Jake. And Jared Cross."

Her heart gathered itself into a knot and cannonballed into her toes. "You talked to Dr. Cross?"

Tabitha looked at her strangely. "He's my director of child psychiatry. I talk to him on a regular basis."

"About *me?*" Her sessions with him were supposed to have been confidential! Or had someone noticed her visiting him? Had rumor gotten out some other way? Tabitha was right about one thing. The hospital-employee environment was closeknit, with people spending long, stress-filled hours together. Gossip was rife.

But Tabitha was shaking her head. "I talked to him about all my staff who were involved in that nightmare. I wanted to know if I could help in any respect."

Cait finally let her air out. That made sense. It was something Tabitha would do.

"And he mentioned that everyone needed to get back on with their lives as expeditiously as possible," Tabitha continued.

Cait nodded. "But I never do balls or that sort of thing."

"I think you should do this one," Tabitha said. "Jake thinks it will be good for you, too. He's expected to be released from the hospital by then. Besides, everyone is talking about you. You should stop in, even for a little while, to show them that you're absolutely fine."

Cait choked on a laugh. "If I showed up at the ball, they'd buzz about it for a week. *That* would be uncharacteristic of me."

"So's a bag full of wine and schnapps, sweetie, but I won't tell anyone."

Cait pressed a hand to her heart. Tabitha was right. She'd been off the wall lately. But she really didn't want the rest of the hospital staff to know that.

"Unplumbed depths," Tabitha reminded her.

Cait blushed. "I'll think about it."

She waved her friend goodbye and meticulously redid all the locks on her door. Then she went back to the kitchen and eyed the bottle of schnapps.

The thought of actually attending a hospital ball had her unscrewing the cap and sipping right from the bottle.

Sam hit the play button on his answering machine one more time and listened to Kimberlie Leon's message as he unknotted the tie from his neck. She was persistent, he thought. He liked that in a woman.

Her voice sounded like smoke. "You cut me off today before I could ask you what I wanted to ask you," she said. "Bad boy."

"That's me," Sam said into the pause.

"I'd like to invite you to attend the End of Summer Ball with me. Being new at the hospital, I'm groping for a date."

"Somehow I doubt that." Sam tossed his tie onto the back of the sofa.

Kimberlie left her number. "If I miss you tonight, catch up with me tomorrow at the hospital. Please?"

"You can bet on it." He finally hit the erase button on his machine.

Houdini barked his appreciation of the coup. He was a somewhat overweight golden retriever. The extra pounds were courtesy of the dogcatcher who picked him up on a regular basis and brought him home from his shenanigans whenever Houdini took it into his canine head to roam the neighborhood. The predilection cost Sam twenty-five dollars a pop. Sam figured that at least half the fee went toward the doggy biscuits the dogcatcher routinely fed Houdini. The two of them were great pals.

The dog barked again.

"Okay, you want to go out." Sam scowled. "Just hold on to your pants for a minute."

He went into his bedroom, dropping clothes on the way. He stepped over a pair of running shoes in the hallway. No big deal. The maid was coming in two days and the place would be spotless again. Besides, he never entertained at home, anyway—at least not women. He figured if he ever invited one here, she'd take it as a sign that he was serious about her.

"Never happen," Sam said aloud. He changed into a pair of gym shorts and a sweatshirt and went back to the kitchen for Houdini's leash, snapping it on to the dog's collar. Then he went barefoot to the door.

As he opened it onto the veranda that fronted all the condominiums on the third floor, the dog surged forward and nearly knocked over Ricky Mercado, who lived next door. "Sorry," Sam said. He reeled Houdini back in. It had taken him months on a waiting list to snag this apartment. On most occasions, when he remembered to care, he didn't want to tick off his neighbors.

Especially neighbors with mob ties. Though, in Mercado's case, that was rumored to be a thing of the past.

"No problem," Ricky said easily enough, unlocking his door. "I'm having a bad night, anyway. A precious little blonde just shot me to my knees."

Sam felt an unseen fist hit his stomach while an image of deep-blue eyes and short blond hair tried to fill up every one of his senses. "Precious little blondes can be trouble."

"Tell me about it." Mercado stopped in his open doorway and laughed. "She was a nurse. I guess the law-abiding type still doesn't go for my reputation."

A nurse? Sam felt something strange happen to his heart. Okay, Mission Creek had its fair share, he thought. But small and blond? "Uh, where did you see her?"

"Outside Signey's Liquor. Why?"

"No reason. I was just curious." Sam breathed again. Not Cait Matthews, then. She was the last woman in the world who'd stop and buy liquor on her way home from work. She was straight as an arrow.

But this one had shot down Ricky Mercado—and

what kind of a woman would do *that?* One who was straight as an arrow, he answered himself.

And Cait had been acting odd lately. Odd enough to be buying liquor, at any rate.

"What was her excuse?" he asked. "Did she even give you one?"

"She said she had plans."

Ricky went into his condo and shut the door. Houdini made a sudden lunge for the stairs and nearly pulled Sam off his feet. He glanced back twice at Mercado's apartment door before he let the dog lead him downstairs.

They reached the enclosed pet area, a five-hundred-square-foot area beside the pool bound by white fencing and signs saying Curb Your Dog in large red lettering.

"Yeah, yeah," Sam said. He opened the gate, let Houdini inside and snapped off the leash. The retriever bounded for the far fence and leaped over it with one strong thrust of his hindquarters. Sam went upstairs to write another check to the animal-control officer.

He didn't think about Caitlyn again until he happened to glance at Ricky Mercado's closed apartment door. A little blonde in a nurse's uniform. The odds were astronomical that the woman had actually been Cait, he told himself.

He let himself inside and went to the kitchen for a beer, peering skeptically at the rest of the refrigerator's contents while he was there. A box of leftover pizza. Two limes from the gin-and-tonics he'd shared with a redhead downstairs at the pool the weekend before his life had hit a major bump, landing him in Branson Hines's basement. With a little blonde in a nurse's uniform.

Okay, he owed it to himself to be sure, didn't he? Even if the odds were really remote.

Sam took the beer back to a living room filled with sleek black leather furniture and plush white carpeting. Houdini—bless his soul—had so far spared the carpeting. The dog liked to do his business in the wide open spaces. Sam picked up the cordless phone on the sofa and hit the on button with his thumb.

Dead as his parents' marriage, he thought, listening for a dial tone, hearing none.

He'd forgotten to recharge it again. He took it to the end table and plugged it into the base there, then went back to the kitchen to use the wall phone. It was red. The last owner had had some serious deficiencies in taste. Sam picked that phone up, then he stalled.

This was not a woman whose number he'd committed to memory. Probably because it had never occurred to him before to call her or anyone like her.

What the hell were her plans tonight, anyway?

"Probably not even the same nurse," he muttered aloud. And why should he care, anyway?

Because, damn it, he really hated to be used as a springboard for some California intern. It was insulting. And why else would Cait have turned down someone like Ricky Mercado unless she was seeing the California intern tonight? Sam hung the telephone up again with a slam and turned around to look for a phone book. Where the maid put it was a mystery likely to remain unsolved for quite some time.

He turned back to the telephone and picked it up

again, calling information. She had an unpublished
listing. He was getting seriously annoyed. Whom did
she chum around with at the hospital? Who might
know her phone number? No one came to mind. But
they'd both spent some significant time with the police a few days ago. Sam finally tapped in the city
number. *That* he knew by heart from retrieving Houdini.

He reached the police department and identified
himself. He told the desk sergeant a tall tale about
his still having Cait's wallet after their ordeal. It had
fallen out of her purse when they'd been escaping,
and he'd stuck it in his own pocket for safekeeping.
He'd only just discovered it. The cop hesitated, then
tried to get him to bring it to the police station. Sam
finessed him, telling him he would take it to the address on her driver's license. He'd just been trying to
avoid showing up at her door unannounced, he lied.
After everything she'd been through, a surprise knock
might alarm her.

The man finally coughed up the number. "I still
got it," Sam murmured, hanging up again. "The old
powers of persuasion." Then he did something he
couldn't remember doing since his fourteenth birth-
day. Reciting the number aloud, he went to a drawer,
got out a fast-food napkin and a pen, and wrote the
number down for future reference.

He went back to the telephone and tapped it in. He
was rewarded for his efforts by a monotonous and
irritating beeping.

Her line was busy. What the hell did that mean?
She was probably talking to Estrada, finalizing their
plans, he realized.

Who cared?

Sam was thoroughly disgusted with himself. He picked up the telephone one last time to call Kimberlie Leon back. He never went to hospital events. They were just an excuse for employees to brownnose their superiors, or for amateurs to get drunk and do stupid things that would haunt them for another two years. But Dr. Leon was a little too enticing to turn down.

Besides, going out with her would take his mind off precious little blondes in nurse's uniforms like nothing else could.

Cait's head was buzzing a little.

She stood in her kitchen, munching on a fortune cookie. In retrospect, she thought, it had been an amazing day. She giggled and reached for the bottle of cactus schnapps again. "Very good stuff," she pronounced. "A woman with unplumbed depths could certainly be expected to appreciate such a thing."

She drank and swallowed, hiccuping a little. She was out of control, she thought again...and she was free.

Something tried to kick inside her chest. Had her mother been drinking cactus schnapps before she'd dumped her two-year-old daughter on an aunt and disappeared for all time?

Cait decided she didn't want any more, after all. She put the schnapps bottle back on the kitchen counter with a loud thud. She hadn't inherited her mother's cold heart or her indifference, she assured herself. If anything, she cared too much about things.

She cared so much that the idea of just being a challenge to Sam Walters cut her to the bone.

Suddenly she was enraged by the thought. She was beside herself with it. She wanted to know. She *had* to know. She went to the telephone and called information.

"I need a number for a Dr. Sam Walters, please."

"Address?" the tinny voice came back.

She hadn't a clue. "It would be somewhere wonderful. Somewhere exotic and flamboyant and—" she paused "—very single-oriented," she decided.

"I have six listings for Walters," the voice responded dryly. "But only one with the initial S."

"Let's try that one."

Cait kept the number in her head while she disconnected and punched it in. His line was busy. He was talking to someone. Probably Dr. Kimberlie Leon.

Suddenly appalled with herself at what she had just done, Cait slammed down the phone as Billy snaked around her ankles, begging for food. What if Sam had actually answered? Fate had spared her ever having to know.

Cait went back to the living room to the pile of books on the coffee table. *This* was her life. She sorted through them, trying to figure out which one she wanted to read next. She selected one, turned on the lamp on the end table and curled her legs under her to open the book on her lap.

Then she put her head down on one of the pillows and promptly fell asleep.

Four

Cait felt like an idiot as she paused on the threshold of the Lone Star Country Club ballroom a week later. What was she doing here? The question reverberated in her head as she teetered a little in the kind of high heels she rarely wore. She gripped her small clutch bag in front of her like a shield against all the potential horrors that could befall her if she actually entered the room.

Where were her unplumbed depths when she needed them?

"Cait!"

She looked around quickly at the sound of Tabitha's voice. Her friend swooped down on her, dragging Jake White by the hand. Tabitha looked gorgeous in strapless, electric-blue satin. *She* didn't seem to have a problem with high heels.

Cait unclenched one hand from her purse and lifted it in a halfhearted wave. "Hi."

"You're certainly looking no worse for wear," Jake said. She hadn't seen him since her rescue from Hines's clutches. To Cait's utter shock, he leaned in and kissed her on the cheek.

"I could say the same for you," she murmured. No one would ever have thought that he'd spent over a week in the hospital. He still looked tall, tough, toned.

She was stunned to find herself actually envying Tabitha a little as the man draped an arm over her friend's shoulders.

"Come on," Tabitha said. "Let's eat, drink and make merry."

Cait moved into the ballroom with them. The place was done in blue and silver, and the chandeliers glinted with dim, golden light. A little path was traced on the carpet between the dance floor and the tables. They followed it to the opposite end of the room where a courtesy bar and buffet were laid out.

Tabitha stopped periodically to talk with her staff, but Jake seemed content just to be alive and in love. "I like the eating part of her suggestion," he said as Tabitha veered off into a conversation with two of her surgeons.

They stepped up to the buffet. Jake speared a cocktail meatball with a pretty toothpick as Cait stared at the array. It was all finger food. She'd been hoping for something more substantial, something that would resemble dinner.

"Is this what they serve at this type of affair?" she asked hesitantly.

"Hey, Tabitha works hard with the budget." Jake winked at her. "These, I believe, are genuine monkey meat. But with the chutney sauce, who can tell?" He popped the meatball into his mouth and chewed.

Cait laughed and liked the feel of it. She filled a small plate with tiny peeled shrimp, then she felt warm breath tickle her neck. "Any woman who looks as good as you do ought to be sipping champagne," said a voice from behind her.

Cait jerked around so quickly a shrimp almost slid off her plate. She caught it. It was Kenny Estrada. "Hi," she said a little breathlessly.

"Dance with me." Kenny took her free hand. "Please."

"I was just—" Cait broke off when Jake took her plate from her "—eating."

"Consider your hors d'oeuvres to be in safekeeping," Jake said.

"Now you have no excuse," Kenny said.

Cait felt her unplumbed depths twitch a little. "Except for one thing. I believe you offered me champagne."

To her absolute amazement and delight, Kenny laughed. The way Ricky Mercado had laughed. Deeply, happily. Cait's pulse kicked.

A waiter passed at just that moment, and Kenny took a flute off the tray, handing it to her. "There you go."

Cait sipped and sighed. The bubbles tickled her lip. "Thank you." Then the band swerved into "Someone to Watch over Me." Cait sighed. She loved old forties music.

"Can you dance with that in your hand?" Kenny asked.

"Of course." Actually, she had no idea. But Cait passed her purse to Jake, as well. "Hold this for me, please?"

She discovered the art of slow-dancing while holding a flute of champagne. It worked, she thought, if you looped your arm around the man's neck just so, without really holding on. Then you could grip the glass, too.

Cait relaxed and began to honestly enjoy herself.

Cait was the first person Sam noticed when he stepped into the ballroom. She wore something in mint green that shimmered. The dress cleaved his tongue to the roof of his mouth and rendered his ears deaf. He saw Kimberlie Leon's lips moving as she spoke to him, but he had no idea what she was saying.

He had no idea because Caitlyn Matthews—every petite, slender inch of her—was wrapped in something skintight, not to mention Kenny Estrada's arms.

As Sam watched, staring, she lifted a glass of champagne over the intern's shoulder. The man laughed and let go of her just long enough for her to take a sip from it. Then he pulled her close again.

"What?" Sam jerked around as Kimberlie's voice finally penetrated his daze with the force of a sonic boom.

She lifted one pretty brow. "I was just saying that I think our table is back that way." She pointed. "Number twenty-two."

"Do you want to sit or do you want to dance?"

She smiled slowly. "Dance. Definitely dance. I've had fantasies for weeks now about finding my way into your arms."

"I can take care of that." Sam got a grip on himself and grinned. As a waiter passed, he plucked a glass of champagne from his tray. Damned if he was going to be outdone by a sparrow of a nurse. "But you'll need this first."

Kimberlie took it and followed him to the dance floor. Then she knocked back half of it and set the glass on a table at the rim of the floor. Sam thought it lacked the finesse of a glass draped around a man's neck, but then she slid into his arms and pressed herself close. He held her, intent on making the most of the moment.

Then he felt his gaze cutting to Cait again.

Had she been seeing Estrada this past week since she had shot down Ricky Mercado? *If* she had shot down Ricky Mercado, he reminded himself. The jury was still out as to whether this little blond nurse was the same one who had bruised Mercado's ego.

The song ended. He watched Cait ease out of Estrada's arms, but then she rested her free hand on his shoulder and murmured something in his ear. The pair moved off to a table.

"Time to eat," Sam decided.

Kimberlie pulled out of his arms to look at him. "Are you serious? We only started dancing."

"I just realized I'm starving."

He led her off the floor in the direction of the bar and the buffet. He glanced at Cait's table as they passed it. Estrada was holding a shrimp out to her. Instead of just taking it from the man's fingers, she opened her mouth and let him lay it on her tongue.

Sam choked.

He dropped Kimberlie's hand and pointed at the laden buffet table. "The food is right over there."

She gaped at him. "You're not coming with me? Eating was your idea."

"Grab something for me. Please?"

She nodded, still looking confused. "Sure."

"I just noticed someone I want to say hello to. I'll meet you back at our table in a minute."

"All right."

Cait looked up from her plate and felt her stomach dive. Sam was approaching her table. The shrimp became clogged in her throat.

"Dr. Walters," she said when he reached her.

"Selective memory," he murmured, pulling out a chair and reaching for one of her shrimp.

Cait slapped his hand before she knew she was going to do it. "Get your own. And what does that mean? Selective memory?"

"It means that apparently you only call me Dr. Walters these days when you're not trying to chop me off at the knees."

Cait's gaze flew to Kenny and her face flamed. "I've never chopped him off at the knees," she said quickly. "He must be drunk."

"Stone sober," Sam disagreed. "We just got here."

"We?" Cait hated herself for asking, but the word was out of her mouth before she could catch it.

"I brought Kimberlie Leon."

"Apparently slammed doors turn her on." Cait felt her heart kick as she wondered where the tart words had come from. Then hurt rained through her from her heart to her toes. He had brought a date. And the date wasn't her. Even though they had done *it* just a few weeks ago.

Then again, what had she expected?

Sam grinned like a shark. "She invited me. What could I do but oblige?"

"Which just goes to show there's no accounting for people's tastes."

"I do believe you're being sarcastic again, Nurse Matthews."

"It's my unplumbed depths."

He laughed. Like Kenny had. Like Ricky Mercado had. Cait felt bemused.

"What unplumbed depths?" Kenny asked.

Sam lowered his voice so only she could hear. "'Show me how.' I'd say that's about as unplumbed as you can get."

Cait had just taken another sip of champagne and it almost came up through her nose. "Don't you have a date to get back to?" She looked at him again, hoping her eyes were shooting daggers.

"She's getting me something to eat."

They both looked at the buffet table at the same time. Kimberlie Leon waggled her fingers at them in greeting.

Sam leaned closer to Cait. "Here's the way these hospital parties go," he said conspiratorially. "Dr. Leon will be seriously intoxicated within the hour. So will Lover Boy sitting there beside you."

"His name is Kenny."

"Whatever."

Cait was appalled. "We're hospital personnel. No one is going to drink too much. Half of them are on call."

"Oh, they will. Take my word for it."

"If you've got such disdain for them, why are you here?"

"Why are you?" he countered.

Because she was seriously trying to get back to

normal, although how something as uncharacteristic for her as a party could help on that score, Cait still didn't know. And she'd die before she'd admit to him that her shrink had recommended it.

Sam took her hand where it rested on the table. "Tell you what. Let's make a run for it and leave these people behind."

Cait jerked her hand free. "You're out of your mind."

"I'm starting to think so."

He looked almost serious, she thought. It made her heart do odd things. "I'm not leaving here with you. You have a date."

"Then just dance with me."

"Next lifetime." She knew, somehow, that if she ever let herself back into his arms again, she would never let go. Her heart started slamming into her ribs.

"Come on, Cait," Kenny said suddenly. "They're playing our song."

Cait looked at him, wondering where he had come from.

Then she registered what he had just said. They didn't have a song. He was rescuing her. She grabbed the hand Kenny held out to her like a lifeline and left Sam sitting at the table, alone. She didn't dare look back.

Tabitha Monroe found her way to Jared Cross's side at the bar. She toasted him and inclined her head in the direction of the scene unfolding at Cait's table. "Interesting," she murmured conversationally.

Cross grinned. "The quiet ones usually are."

"Spoken like a true shrink," Tabitha said just as

Melanie Tourbier approached and tucked her hand into Jared's arm. "Personally, my theory is that the arrogant ones always meet their match."

"And you were speaking of...?"

Tabitha blinked innocently at Cross. "Sam Walters, of course."

"Of course."

"What do you suppose happened between them in that basement room?" Tabitha wondered aloud.

"I'm sure that if Nurse Matthews confided in anyone, it would be privileged."

Tabitha looked at him. "You don't know, either."

"Nope." Cross handed his drink to Melanie as Cait and Kenny Estrada danced. "I'll be back in a few minutes. I want to check in with her and see if she's doing okay."

Tabitha pounced on that. "She *is* seeing you professionally." She'd thought so, if only because of Cait's reaction the other night when she'd mentioned Cross. "Good. I approve of that."

Cross glanced back at her. "I'm just acting in a friendly capacity."

In a pig's eye, Tabitha thought. "What about Sam?"

"He can take care of himself."

The dance ended, and Cait and Kenny began to make their way to Cait's table. Tabitha and Melanie watched Sam Walters launch himself up from that same table and stalk to his own. He took a startled Kimberlie Leon by the hand just as she was about to swallow her first bite of food. He pulled her to her feet and onto the dance floor. Dr. Leon was starting to look mutinous.

Melanie and Tabitha tapped their glasses together in a silent toast.

"This," Tabitha said, "is going to be fun to watch."

When Cait returned to her table after the dance, she saw Jared Cross sitting there this time. Something inside her hitched and she glanced quickly at Kenny. She didn't want to talk to Dr. Cross in front of him. Not that she didn't trust Jared to be utterly professional. She just wasn't quite sure of her own tongue these days.

"Could you get me another glass of champagne?" she asked the intern.

Kenny looked startled. "You haven't finished your first one yet."

Her initial foray into the world of alcoholic beverages a week ago had left her feeling a little muddleheaded the next day. She'd discovered that she didn't have much capacity for alcohol and so had determined never, ever to repeat the experience. "It's going a little flat," she said. Heaven knew she'd nursed it long enough.

When Kenny agreed and turned away, she joined Jared. "So, Doctor, am I performing to your satisfaction?"

A small smile touched his mouth. "Was that sarcasm I just heard from you?"

Cait sat. "Yes, I believe so."

"I just wanted to see how you were doing with all this." He waved a hand at the room.

Cait's gaze skittered over the gathering. "I never do parties. I don't see how this can possibly help me get back to normal. But actually…I'm enjoying my-self a little."

"The party isn't the point," Cross explained. "The people are. It's from the same school of thought that said you needed to go back to that storage room last week."

Cait quickly sipped flat champagne. All the storeroom had gotten her was titillated. She squirmed a little in her seat.

"It's a common symptom of post-traumatic stress disorder to avoid any reminder of the traumatic incident," Cross explained.

"I know." She had spent the better part of the past week assiduously dodging contact with any of the employees who'd escaped through the vent before she and Sam were abducted. And she hadn't spoken to any of them tonight, either, though they were all here.

"Since you refused to join in the group therapy I recommended, I thought this would be the next best thing," Cross continued.

The very thought of opening up to a roomful of strangers made her itchy. "Are you implying that I…I should interact with these people?" she asked carefully.

"It wouldn't hurt."

"But would it help?"

"In all likelihood, yes."

She looked around and steeled herself for it. Then she heard Cross sigh. She glanced back at him. "What?"

"Caitlyn, I'm not suggesting that you face a firing squad."

"Close enough." She bit the words out through a tight jaw.

"You sell yourself short."

She was startled. "How?"

"You're a witty, clever, beautiful woman. People enjoy being around you when you give them the chance."

Cait felt her jaw drop. She pulled herself together again. "I'm not insecure. I just don't need a lot of...other people in my life."

"Why not?"

This was starting to feel like one of her appointments with him. "I'm better off by myself."

"Where you have control over everything that happens to you? Fewer variables that way?"

She flushed. "Well...yes."

Cross laughed. Then he sobered. "That's a logical reaction to your childhood, Caitlyn."

"I keep telling you—"

He held up a hand. "I know, I know. No one was ever unkind to you."

She nodded, somewhat mollified. The only truly bad moment she could remember was the time she'd been uprooted from one home in the middle of the night, wakened by a social worker from a dead sleep in the darkness and whisked off to another home. Years later she'd learned that it was because her foster mother had committed suicide in the next room. The authorities had been trying to spare her the sight. All the same, she'd been terrified at the time.

It was why her apartment was so important to her, why she paid her rent months in advance. Nothing like that would ever happen to her again.

"Likewise," said Cross, "your reaction to this ordeal—in the face of your past—is utterly predictable."

Cait straightened. "I don't think I like being predictable."

"But you are."

Not lately. It was as if something inside her was rebelling, she thought. All her predictability and orderliness hadn't saved her from Hines, after all.

"You're actually doing very well," Cross said. "A lot of people suffering PTSD even exhibit physical symptoms."

Cait blinked at him. "Like what?"

"Headaches, nausea, backaches, missed periods."

Cait shook her head. "No, I haven't experienced any of—"

Then she broke off as her heart rolled over. It dawned on her in that moment that her period was a couple of days late.

Something start to shake inside her. It was just as Dr. Cross had said, she assured herself. It was a physical reaction to her ordeal. The hostage situation had seriously gotten to her. She was still so addled by it that she hadn't even realized she was late until just this moment! And she was *always* prepared, always armed with her calendar, because she was exceptionally regular.

Cait covered her face with her hands. She was falling apart. Even her body was betraying her now.

"Are you all right?" Kenny asked as he returned to their table and placed a glass of champagne in front of her.

She looked up again quickly. "I'm fine." Her

heart was thundering. She was going to be sick. What if she had gotten pregnant in that underground room?

How much further out of control could her life spin?

Cait leaped to her feet. Kenny and Jared stared at her.

"What is it?" Jared asked.

"I...I think I left a candle burning at home." It was the first thing that came to her mind.

"Is there a neighbor you can call?" Cross asked, concerned.

"I...no." She shook her head and ran her fingers nervously through her hair. "I have to go."

"I'll give you a lift," Kenny offered. "We can check it out and come back."

"No," she said again, and even she heard the thin reed of desperation in her voice. "That's not necessary." Cait grabbed her purse and fled.

"Your friend seems upset," Kimberlie Leon said to Sam on the dance floor.

He looked around quickly, just in time to see roughly a hundred pounds of trim and glittering mint-green sail out the ballroom door. He'd been trying hard to keep his mind off her. Now something kicked him hard in the chest. Something was wrong. He unwrapped his arms from Kimberlie's voluptuous body.

"I'll be right back," he said.

"What's wrong with you tonight, anyway?" she demanded.

Sam looked at her, surprised. "Nothing's wrong with me."

She had her hands on her hips now and looked

very unhappy. "Well, I'm here to tell you that you're *nothing* like what they said."

"Like who said?" He was genuinely dumbfounded. "Why not?"

"Rumor had it that you could make a woman feel like a million dollars. I feel like chump change!"

Sam was seriously appalled. He didn't want *that* getting out. "I'm sorry."

"Then finish dancing with me." She held her arms out to him again.

He glanced at the ballroom door. Cait was long gone, but maybe he could still catch up with her outside. It would take the valet a few minutes to get her car. "I can't." He left Kimberlie and started off the dance floor.

"Who is she, anyway?" Kimberlie shouted after him angrily.

"Just some sparrow," he muttered under his breath. One who had somehow managed to get under his skin while he hadn't been paying attention. He hurried out into the corridor and to the staircase leading downstairs.

He jogged outside just as her car sped away down the circular drive. He swore aloud.

"Would you like your car, sir?" the valet asked.

"No." His voice was a frustrated growl. He'd missed her by seconds. His heart was still moving hard.

Sam turned back inside. He was going to have to do something about this. About this situation. About *her.* Unfortunately he had no idea what.

When he got back to the ballroom, Kimberlie Leon was dancing with Kenny Estrada. Sam wasn't surprised.

The woman was seated at a table by herself at the far end of the ballroom. Her pathetic excuse for a date had gone to get her another drink.

His timing had actually been perfect. If she'd been preoccupied with him, she might not have noticed what was going on with little Nurse Matthews. Then again, a portion of her attention had been on her—and on Sam Walters—all night.

Something was afoot, she decided, something interesting. She had never been above using another person's weaknesses or problems for her own gain, but in this case she couldn't imagine what Caitlyn Matthews's obvious upset might mean to her. She pursed her lips, thinking about it. One minute the little twit had been talking to Jared Cross, then that slick intern had come back and she'd jumped up to run. The woman doubted the intern had had anything to do with it. But she'd put money on it having been something that Dr. Cross had said.

As for Sam, he hadn't taken his eyes off Caitlyn all night. And Kimberlie Leon was one seriously ticked-off doctor. The woman laughed aloud at that.

Hospitals weren't altogether bad places, after all.

There was only one way to find out what was going on, she decided, eyeing her date as he headed back toward their table. Poor little Nurse Matthews obviously needed a friend, someone she could confide in.

"Here you go," her date said, offering her a fresh drink.

The woman took it and grinned like a cat.

Five

Cait didn't even make it home without stopping at an all-night drugstore.

"You're being an absolute ninny," she said to herself through clenched teeth, sitting behind the wheel of her car after she parked. "It's just two days." But she was never late. Her body had always been as orderly as the rest of her life.

Cait had a sudden mental image of a firecracker spiraling crazily out of control. That was all that was left of her old self these days, she thought desperately—a bunch of errant, fizzling sparks. *Pregnant?*

She had to know, and as soon as possible. There was no sense in going off the deep end until she had the facts. But she needed them immediately. If she was pregnant, she had to start taking better care of herself. Not that she hadn't always done so before. She was very careful about her cholesterol—after all, her great-aunt, the only relative she knew anything about, had died of a heart attack. She took multivitamins daily, never neglected a flu shot. But if she was pregnant, then these ridiculous PTSD symptoms were simply going to have to go away.

She groaned aloud and got out of her car. She went inside and stood staring at the intimidating array of pregnancy test kits. Suddenly she had a flash of the liquor store again, of all those bottles of wine and liquors. First booze, now a pregnancy test, she thought giddily. What was next?

She read the back of each box carefully. It was difficult because her hands were shaking and the print kept jumping. Again and again she squeezed her eyes shut and opened them, forcing herself to focus. She finally found what she wanted, one that claimed to give an accurate answer even if a woman was only a day late.

Cait turned to the cash register with it. She waited, her heart leaping in her chest like a rabbit, half expecting the cashier to make some mention of what she was buying. But the girl was clearly not interested. Cait paid for the test and snatched up the bag, then forced herself to walk calmly from the store.

Billy the Kid was lying in the living-room window when she let herself into her apartment, waiting and watching for her as he always did. He looked around when she came in, feigning disinterest, and that was an old trick, too. Then he attempted to roll over on the sill. With a panicked squawk and a thud, he landed on the floor.

Cait dropped the bag and ran to him. "Oh, Billy. Poor baby." She caught him just as he was about to jump up and run away. She stroked his orange fur, crooning to him. "This has been hard on you, too, hasn't it? You were wrapped in a baby blanket, shot at, and now I've disrupted your routine." He looked at her, his eyes accusing, as if to say, *You never go out at night. It's dark out there and you're just coming in. What's this about?*

"I'm sorry," she apologized automatically. Then

she had another staggering thought. What would a baby do to poor Billy's life? And what if she let her baby roll off the window ledge?

Cait pressed her fingers to her temples. What was she thinking? Babies didn't lie on window ledges! Okay, then, a bassinet. Or a changing table. She couldn't handle a baby if she was wacky like this, she thought again. She had to calm down, had to get back to herself. Yes, she thought, this PTSD nonsense was definitely going to have to go.

Cait stood and went back for the bag she'd dropped. She took it into her bathroom, pulled the box out and set it carefully on top of the toilet so it would be readily available in the morning. Ten minutes later she lay in bed, her eyes deliberately closed. Then she jackknifed into a sitting position, letting out an involuntary squeal.

What about Sam?

He'd made it clear what he thought of her. He'd obviously considered her to be nothing more than an amusing diversion while they'd been held captive. He wouldn't want the responsibility of a child, wouldn't want anything to do with it. He was the most emphatic bachelor she had ever met. What if he tried to make her get rid of the baby? Or what if she was misreading him completely and he nosed his way in on the whole business?

A baby would disrupt her life enough, Cait thought. Babies did what they wanted, when they wanted and how they wanted. They did not listen to reason. She couldn't even comprehend what the inclusion of Sam Walters in the mix would do to her world.

''Get hold of yourself,'' she hissed. She didn't even know yet if it was true, if she *was*…pregnant.

Even thinking the word made her stomach somersault all over again. She realized that she literally felt ill, the way she had before going into the hospital for the first time after her ordeal. Cait clapped a hand to her mouth. It was psychosomatic, she assured herself. Her nerves—and her wild mental rantings—were making her sick to her stomach. Or maybe it was as simple as those sips of champagne on a mostly empty stomach. It probably had nothing to do with being…with being…

''Pregnant,'' she whispered.

There, she'd said it aloud. And though her heart thrummed, it didn't actually arrest.

But what about Sam?

If she was pregnant, then she could never, ever let him know, she decided. Something squeezed in the area of her chest, but she knew it was the best thing she could do. She would change jobs, move to another city. What really held her in Mission Creek, after all? She'd been alone her whole life; she could raise a child that way, as well. She just couldn't do it here, right under Sam's nose.

Cait lay back down carefully and closed her eyes again. It wasn't until she was dozing off that her whirling thoughts finally settled into something a little more coherent. It occurred to her that in all her wild ramblings, every panic-ridden possibility involved keeping the baby.

Cait was awake before the alarm went off the next day. She hurried into the bathroom at first light, trip-

ping over Billy on the way. He let out an indignant
yowl and fled into the living room. She forgot to go
after him to tell him that she was sorry. She closed
and locked the bathroom door, forgetting, too, that
she lived alone and no one was likely to intrude.

Then she did the test.

Cait carried the little stick back to the bedroom
and placed it on her dresser. Then she sat on her bed
and watched the nightstand clock. One minute passed
with excruciating deliberation. Time crawled. She
whimpered with frustration.

Two minutes. Three. It was finally time to look at
the stick, but she found that she couldn't get up from
the bed to go see.

Another full minute passed before Cait managed
to stand. She crept to the dresser. Closed her eyes.
Looked down. Opened them again.

Positive.

She gave a small cry of distress and felt her knees
start to fold. She grabbed the stick and ran to the
bathroom to get the carton and compare the stick to
the picture there. A pink line meant positive. It was
definitely positive.

Well, then.

Suddenly a quiet sense of calm and wonder stole
over her. She could do this, she realized again. It was
really just a matter of organizing, planning, getting
her life in the proper order to accommodate a new-
born. And she had nine whole months to do that.
Well, eight and a half. But organizing was something
she was very good at. It wouldn't take her that long.

She put a hand to her tummy. A baby. Someone

to belong to, who would belong to her. Finally. It was overwhelming. Her throat closed.

She finally dropped the box and the stick into the trash can. Within half an hour she had showered and dressed in jeans and a pink T-shirt. She sat at her kitchen table and dutifully shoveled in spoonfuls of cornflakes.

A baby.

She read the nutritional values on the back of the cereal box avidly. It might be time to take a step up from the generic brand, she thought. She would have to compare the vitamin percentages the next time she was in the grocery store.

But her first order of business was Sam.

Cait took her bowl to the sink and rinsed it out. She had to put as much space between them as possible and as soon as possible. Her heart squeezed. They'd worked together for four years. He knew her well, at least in a professional capacity. What if her behavior tipped him off? If she suddenly felt repeatedly queasy or light-headed, he would notice. She could hardly be running to the bathroom every ten minutes to toss up her cookies without him wondering why.

Cait found her car keys and drove to the hospital.

This time she didn't hesitate as she parked and went inside. She was a woman with a mission. She went directly to the personnel office and sat, flipping through a magazine, until a counselor came out of one of the back rooms. She was a statuesque blonde in a ruby-red blouse and trim denim jeans. She looked surprised to see Cait. "Can I help you?"

Cait put the magazine down quickly. "Yes, please. I need to speak to someone about a transfer."

"Well, go on back to my office. What's your name? I'll get your file."

Cait told her and went back to the only room with an open door and lights on. She sat and waited for the woman to return.

When the counselor did, she dropped a blue folder on her desk and sat behind it neatly. "A transfer, hmm?"

Cait nodded. "To another physician. I'm an RN here."

"Yes."

Cait was startled. "It's that easy? I can have a transfer just like that?"

"Well, pretty much. But what I meant was, yes, I know you're an RN. I've glanced at your file. I'm Nancy Walters, by the way."

Cait smiled politely and nodded, then her heart jumped over a beat. "Walters?"

The woman smiled. "Bingo. I was married to Sam Walters, a physician on staff here. The one you apparently want to be reassigned from. Does that make this awkward?"

Yes, Cait thought. No. "Oh, my. I didn't realize you work here." And she'd never heard that Sam had been married. Then again, she tried to stay away from gossip.

"I only started a few months ago," Nancy explained. "If you like, I can hold your file for another counselor. Emmy Metican will be in tomorrow. I just stopped in to catch up on some things. That's the only reason you caught me here on a weekend."

Cait felt herself flushing. "That won't be necessary," she said, deciding. "Let's get this over with."

Nancy nodded and pulled a green form out of a drawer. "Are you having a problem with Sam?"

"No," Cait said quickly. She realized suddenly that if she said anything negative about him, his exwife could use it against him if she wanted to hurt him. Maybe this was a bad idea, after all.

"We're still friends," Nancy said as though reading her mind. "Plus, I like my alimony."

"Ah." Cait gave a shaky laugh.

"It's just that, in instances like this, I need to give a reason for the request."

"That makes sense."

Nancy waited a moment. "And yours would be?" she asked finally.

"Oh!" Cait opened her mouth, closed it, then opened it again. "Well, we were kidnapped together."

The woman's expression turned from one of wry humor to compassion. "Yes, I heard about it. Everyone has."

Cait flinched, reminded of how Tabitha had said everyone was talking about her. "The whole ordeal was painful for me." Her mind seized on the word Dr. Cross often used. "It was traumatic."

"I'm sure it was."

"I want to start over. I…I want to transfer to neonatal." She hadn't considered it before, but the words just popped out.

"To the nursery? That's where it happened, in the new wing, right?"

Cait nodded hard. "Yes."

"Wouldn't that be difficult for you, as well?"

"Actually, it's the people associated with the nightmare that I'm having trouble with, not the location. I went back there last week. I was fine." Then she thought of the things Sam had said that day and felt her face flame.

Nancy nodded and pretended not to notice. "Some of the people who escaped work in that unit," she reminded her.

Cait thought fast. "That's just it. *They* escaped."

"But you and Sam didn't."

"Exactly. It's no personal reflection on him at all—or professional, either, for that matter. I've worked with him for years. He's a good doctor. But I need a clean slate now." She was talking too much, Cait realized. She was babbling. But she badly needed to convince this woman to put in for the transfer. "I want to be able to do my job without constant reminders," she continued. "And...and Dr. Walters is the only one who seems to remind me of what happened."

Nancy sat back. "It sounds reasonable to me, but I'm not a psychiatrist."

"I'm trained in pediatrics," Cait pointed out.

Nancy nodded. "Okay. I'll put in the request for you."

Cait breathed again. "How long will it take?"

"If there's an opening—and I don't know yet because I'd have to run it through the computer—it could be just a matter of days."

That sounded good, Cait thought. She rose to her feet. "Thank you."

Nancy reached to shake her hand. "You're welcome."

Cait turned away, then the woman's voice froze her. "You must be a special woman. You put up with Sam for quite awhile."

Cait jerked back to look at her. "Damn it, nothing happened!"

Nancy looked shocked, then confused, then curious. Cait realized that the counselor had been speaking professionally. She felt color flood to the roots of her hair this time, and she fled the office without another word.

Things just kept getting more interesting, the woman thought.

She watched Caitlyn Matthews hustle down the hospital's main corridor in her oh-so-white sneakers and her saccharin-sweet pink top. Then her curiosity turned to anger. Something painful punched her between the eyes from the inside out.

So the twit had a problem she thought personnel could fix. It just made the woman more determined to find out what was going on.

At the end of the hallway, Caitlyn stopped, rubbed the back of her neck and looked over her shoulder. The woman quickly stepped into a doorway, out of sight.

Sam got the emergency call from the hospital at two o'clock Sunday afternoon. Gilbert Travalini was having a rejection episode. Minor, as such things went, but it needed his attention.

Sam was almost glad. It would save him from his parents.

He thumbed the off button on the portable phone, disconnecting the switchboard's call as he sprawled on the sofa and watched a ball game. Then he tapped in his parents' number and spoke to his mother. She was disappointed that he wouldn't be able to make dinner. Maribel Walters lived for Sunday nights when at least one of her children would arrive to share the meal with them. Sam thought it was probably because they spared her the usual silence of her dinner table. She and Sam's father had run out of conversation years ago.

Sam wondered, as he always did, why they hadn't just divorced, instead of producing five kids and dutifully clothing them, feeding them and educating them for the next thirty years or so. And why, when those kids were all fed, clothed and educated, they didn't just shake hands and part ways. He wondered why people got married at all.

The thought depressed him.

By the time he took a shower and arrived at the hospital, his back felt knotted with tension, just as it had since Cait had run out of the ballroom last night. He examined Gil and adjusted the boy's medication. He put an alert on his chart that someone should call him immediately if his fever climbed even one-tenth of a degree higher. Then, because he was in the hospital, anyway, he stopped at his office and scooped out the wad of memos in the clear plastic folder attached to his door.

He winced a little at the one from Kimberlie Leon telling him not to ever call her again. As if he did so with any regularity, Sam thought. He'd done it once—and then it had only been to return *her* call. She'd been the one to instigate the fiasco of the ball last night. *She* had invited *him*.

All the same, he let himself into his office to use the phone to send her flowers with an apology for cutting out early. He leafed through the rest of his memos while the florist had him on hold. When he saw the lime-green personnel slip, he frowned. What the hell? He and Nancy had peacefully coexisted in the hospital for a few months now. To say they'd parted amicably after the divorce was an understatement. Their parents were still the best of friends. But they didn't send memos back and forth between each other.

Sam read this one. It wasn't personal. It was business. Cait had requested a transfer to another physician.

"Thank you for holding," a voice chirped in his ear. Sam slammed the phone down without responding.

What did she want a transfer for? For that matter, the reason she'd bolted from the dance last night was still a mystery to him. He'd asked both Jared Cross and the intern she'd danced with, but neither man had had an answer for him. Estrada had said something inane about a candle.

And now she wanted to work with a different doctor?

Sam shot to his feet, clutching the memo. Something hot tweaked his nerve endings. Because, he thought, she was the best nurse he'd ever had. And how could she abandon Gil Travalini this way? Or any of the other kids who loved her, for that matter?

He found himself downstairs, banging a fist on the personnel-office door, before it dawned on him that it was Sunday. There was no answer. Nancy would be at home, though she had obviously been here at some point today.

Conveniently, he knew where she lived. He sent her an alimony check on the fifth of every month.

Sam jogged outside to his car and revved the engine. The rumbling roar matched his mood. He shot the Maserati into gear and punched the gas. The car lunged out of the parking lot.

His ex-wife lived on a pretty side street in a Spanish-style adobe house half the size of the one they'd shared when they'd been married. She'd gotten their house, of course, in the divorce. She'd been a debutante, he a resident when they'd married. They'd stayed together for three years. In the second year, he'd started earning some significant money. They'd left their rented apartment and purchased a sprawling four-bedroom Mediterranean on the edge of town, near the Carson and Wainwright ranches. Then they'd parted ways and Nancy had pretty much soaked him.

She'd sold the house to buy something smaller and had no doubt invested the difference wisely. Her father was a stockbroker. She also had his alimony payments to live on. Why she felt compelled to work at the hospital was beyond Sam's understanding.

Her Acura was in the driveway. Sam roared to a stop behind it and got out to stalk to the door and rap his knuckles against it. Nancy opened it wearing half a T-shirt and tiny denim shorts. Her feet were bare. She'd painted her toenails to match her fingernails.

There was a reason he had married her. She still looked delicious. It was just that at some point he had started appreciating her without wanting her.

"Hey," he said by way of greeting.

She brought a crimson-colored drink to her mouth and sipped on the straw. "Aren't we a little beyond surprise visits, Sam?"

"It's business. I need to talk to you."

"You could have called." She gave the pout he remembered so well.

"I was already on the road so I just came over. Can I come in or do you have company?"

"Not yet."

He got the hint. "This won't take long," he promised.

She sighed and stepped back from the door to let him into a neutral living room done in Navajo prints. She'd always had good taste and this place was no exception. She put her drink down on a coaster on the coffee table. "This is about Caitlyn Matthews, right?"

Sam crossed his arms. "Well, I'm curious about what's going on here. You saw her today. I got your memo."

Nancy tapped a finger against her lip as she thought about it. "Maybe she has a case of Sam-Walters-Strikes-Again."

Sam dropped his arms, stung. "What's that supposed to mean?"

"You're a great guy, Sam, but you're no kind of husband."

"Cait wants a *husband?*" He was shocked. Then he remembered that she'd been a virgin. "I think I need to sit down."

Nancy watched him as he dropped onto the sofa. "I have no idea if she does or not. What happened between you two in that underground room, anyway?"

"Nothing!" He scrubbed his face, then repeated the word more calmly. "Nothing."

"Well, maybe there's your problem. Maybe you should have zapped her with some of that patented Sam sex appeal. Maybe she's feeling left out."

"Nancy…" He chastised her with his eyes.

She threw her hands in the air. "I'm just saying that was always one thing you were very good at."

If he was so good at it, then why was Cait bailing out on him? "Thanks for that."

"You're welcome. You make a woman feel like a million dollars."

"Or chump change, depending on my mood."

"Pardon me?"

"Never mind."

She sighed and sat beside him. "Sam, you're just no good at monogamy."

He knew that.

"Or order," she added.

Which was why he was no possible match for Cait Matthews, he thought, why he had to get her off his mind. It was for her own sake. A man like him would drive her nuts after a while.

Of course, she was already acting somewhat wacky in his estimation.

Then he thought about it for a minute and finally asked Nancy a question he knew he should have asked a long time ago. "Did I hurt you? When it ended?"

"Of course not." She shook her head, her blond hair skimming her shoulders. "We both saw the writing on the wall and acted accordingly. Anything too closely resembling your father's life gives you hives, and I understand that."

It was more than that, he thought. He'd been passionately in love with Nancy at first, something he doubted his father had ever felt for his mother; what they'd shared had been nothing like his parents' union. He just hadn't been able to hold on to the feeling. It had waned and when it had, he'd been miserable. Nancy had known it, and she'd let him go.

He'd never subjected another woman to that side of himself again and he didn't intend to start now. He never made promises. He knew himself. Or at least he had, until he'd kissed Cait Matthews.

"Did she say why she wanted a transfer?" he asked finally.

Nancy looked confused, then her expression cleared. "Ah, we're off the marriage topic and back to your nurse."

"Sorry. I thought we were finished with the other issue."

Nancy stood again. "We were. Years ago."

"Then tell me why my nurse asked for a transfer."

"I can't. It's confidential."

"Oh, come on. This is me you're talking to."

"You're a hospital employee and I like my job."

"What, you think I'm going to tell on you?"

"Or she will."

"I won't tell her you told me." Then something struck him, a possible reason for Nancy's reticence. "Did she lodge a complaint against me?"

Nancy looked amused. "No. As a matter of fact, she went out of her way to make it clear that it had nothing to do with you. She just wants a change of scenery."

"Why?"

"It seems to have something to do with that ordeal you two went through together."

The ordeal? Or the sex? His heart did something odd. It almost felt as if it spasmed. "That's no reason to throw the baby out with the bathwater."

Nancy looked at her watch. "Sam, I have a friend coming over shortly. I suggest you take it up with Ms. Matthews if you're unhappy with the situation."

"I will." Or he would, if he had any idea where to find her on a Sunday. Sam stood again and headed for the door, then he paused. "Give me your key to the personnel office."

Nancy backed up, waving her hands in front of her as though to ward him off. "Oh, no. No way."

"This is important. I'll copy it and bring it right back to you."

"You're going to try to find out where she lives!"

He didn't bother to deny it.

"Sam, you can't go through your whole life acting as though rules were only made for other people."

"I follow rules!"

"In the hospital, sure," she said. "When you're working. Until now. This is hospital business."

"Right. And I'm a doctor there. Is there any specific rule that says I can't check the file of a nurse who works for me?"

She relented. "Okay, damn it. But don't you dare copy the key. I want to find it in my mailbox when I leave here for work tomorrow morning."

"You will. I promise."

"Just leave it there in the box. Don't knock on my door. Don't try to come in. I'll have company."

"Who is it? Anybody I know?"

"None of your business."

"Someone from the hospital?"

"Same as above."

"Okay, just give me the key."

"I hate you."

"No, you don't." Though maybe, he thought again, she should.

He took the key and left the pretty adobe house he'd paid for. He gunned the car and headed back to the hospital. Fifteen minutes later he had Cait's address.

He had never gone to this much trouble over a woman in his life.

Part of him just wanted to drive home again and forget the whole thing. If she wanted a transfer, let her go. Nurses were a dime a dozen. Good ones... okay, those were harder to come by. But he'd find one eventually.

He glanced at the slip of paper again where he'd scrawled her address. It was a residential street halfway between the hospital and Nancy's home, where he had to go, anyway, to return the key. Instead of turning north toward his condo, Sam kept driving.

Cait was sautéeing sweet red peppers with a little garlic and olive oil when the unexpected knock came at her door. Water was boiling for the linguine. She sighed and turned the burners off, lifting the skillet away from the heat for good measure.

Tabitha could be long-winded.

She headed for the living room, then realized she hadn't washed her hands when she'd left the kitchen. She wiped her palms on the seat of her jeans before grasping the doorknob, then she laughed giddily. She was definitely losing her mind. And why not? Life as she knew it had been turned upside down.

She opened the door and her jaw dropped.

"What the hell are you doing here?" she demanded.

Sam looked shocked. "Did you just swear?"

"Of course not."

"Yeah, you did. You said 'hell.'"

She had, she realized. She pulled herself together. "And you didn't answer my question."

"Don't do that," he said, bracing a hand against the doorjamb.

"Don't do what?" Cait eyed his hand. She couldn't close the door now without severing his fingers.

"That thing with your chin. I really hate it when you do that thing with your chin." He imitated her, bringing his own up a notch.

"You came here to insult me?"

"No. I came here to find out why you don't want to work with me anymore."

Nancy Walters. Cait wasn't sure if she was furious or just felt stupid for trusting the woman. "Your ex-wife called you and told you already."

"I stopped by the hospital to check on Gil Travalini. The memo was in my mail slot."

Cait's heart started beating again slowly. Now what was she supposed to do? Somehow—naively, she realized now—she'd thought the whole thing could go through without any sort of confrontation.

"Well?" he prodded. "Are you going to give me an answer or not?"

"Not. Goodbye." She shut the door, deciding she didn't give a damn about his fingers, after all.

He yelled and jerked them free just in time. "What the hell is wrong with you?" he shouted.

Cait poked her nose through the slit in the door. "Did you just swear?"

"Yeah, but I do it as a matter of course." He was still examining his knuckles, looking aggrieved.

"Sam..." She broke off when he looked at her sharply. "What?" she asked suspiciously.

"You just did it again. You called me Sam. Last night it was Dr. Walters."

"Last night we were at a hospital function. Today you're standing on my doorstep."

"I wouldn't be if you'd let me in so we could talk about this."

"That's not going to happen."

"I want to talk."

"Well, I don't."

"You owe me an explanation."

"I don't believe I do."

"We've worked together for years."

"But not for much longer." She shut the door. He pounded his fist against it again and she pulled it open. "Will you please go away?"

"I will after you tell me why."

Cait sucked in a breath. That was never going to happen. She put a protective hand to her tummy, realized she was doing it and snatched it away. "My reasons are personal."

"We got pretty personal in Hines's underground room, so that should let me in."

Her heart staggered. If he only knew.

In the end, he'd given her a gift unlike any other. Oh, yes, she wanted this baby, she thought. Sam was just a wrinkle in the whole fabric that she needed to eliminate. Before he could whisper more things at her like "Dance with me." Before he could make her laugh again…and make her believe that he meant anything he said or did.

"That," she said quietly, "was a one-time thing." This time when she shut the door, she threw all the locks.

She waited a long time to hear his footsteps go back down the stairs. And finally, at long last, she heard his car engine come to life. Shaky, she went to the window to peer out. He was just sitting behind the wheel, looking confused and lost, and for a moment her heart went out to him. She'd hurt him. And she couldn't bear it.

But that was ridiculous. No woman had the power to hurt Sam—certainly not her, a one-time thing.

He finally backed out of the driveway and left.

When her adrenaline stopped pumping, Cait felt her limbs go to water.

She moved to the sofa and sank onto it, feeling wobbly. She really did have to put some distance between them. She wasn't sure if she could stand much more of seeing Dr. Sam Walters.

Then something itchy moved over her skin again. Hating herself for it, Cait gave in to the urge and went back to the window to look out. This time someone *was* watching her, sort of. It was Mrs. Brody, standing on her back porch. She looked between Cait's apartment and the disappearing Maserati again and again and again.

Cait sighed and went outside to mollify her landlady. She might be a changed woman, but the idea of annoying Mrs. Brody with a rumbling sports car troubled her. She was not about to leave this apartment on anything but her own terms.

Six

Sam drove into the employees' area on Monday morning and found himself parked smack-dab next to Cait's little blue teacup on wheels. He realized it when he got out of his own car, and he glared at it as though it had run over his toes.

First, he thought, she'd acted as though nothing they had done in that basement room had made any difference to her whatsoever. Then she'd gotten all flushed and rattled in the storage room when he'd talked about it, so he'd decided that it really had affected her, after all. Yesterday she'd sent him from her door as cool and calm as you please. He couldn't figure her out. Never, not once, had Sam met a woman who was able to so completely stymie him this way.

He had to remedy this situation. He left her car and stalked toward the hospital entrance. Halfway there, the answer occurred to him.

He wanted to stop in midstride and shout, "Eureka!" Instead, he kept going, grinning now, instead of frowning. Returning to the storage room hadn't gotten her off his mind, and as far as Sam was concerned, Doc Cross should just keep treating childhood hang-ups because he was seriously shaky in the area of post traumatic stress disorder. Therefore, Sam thought, it was time to take matters into his own hands.

Just as Nancy had once said, the single thing that had always managed to take the bloom off the rose for him with any woman was sustained proximity. As a general rule, familiarity bred contempt. Or, at least, it bred disinterest. Therefore, what he needed to get Cait off his mind was…well, more of her.

"Consider yourself about to be seduced, you pretty little nurse," he muttered aloud as he went inside.

He arrived on the pediatrics floor at exactly eight o'clock and found no sign of her. He stopped at the nurses' station. Angelina Moffit was at the computer station there.

"Where's Nurse Matthews?" he asked her.

The woman ignored him.

"Excuse me," Sam tried again.

Angelina looked up. "I'm sorry. Did you say something?"

"I'm looking for Nurse Matthews," he repeated. Then he realized that he could no longer tell what color Angelina's eyes were because they were covered with frost.

She yawned, then she turned to the other side of the semicircular desk, giving him her back. "Hey, Kenny," she said. "Can I help you with something?"

Sam looked that way. Estrada! The intern. Now he understood what was happening here.

Estrada had moved right in on Kimberlie Leon when Sam had found himself out of sorts at the party the other night. That had been after little Nurse I'm-Not-Interested-Maybe-I-Am-No-I'm-Not-After-All had fled the ball without so much as leaving him a slipper to go on. Estrada was obviously the hospital's new bachelor of the hour, Sam realized.

He decided he'd concentrate on getting his ground back in that quarter later. Just as soon as he found Cait.

He turned away from the nurses' station and nearly plowed into Tabitha Monroe.

"Sam," she said. "I need five minutes of your time."

"Sure. Right after rounds." He stepped around her.

"Couldn't we squeeze it in now?" she asked.

"There's something I have to do first." He took two more steps, then stopped and looked back at her. Cait was at least somewhat cozy with the hospital administrator. Or so rumor had it. With Cait it was hard to be sure. "Have you seen Nurse Matthews?" he asked her.

Something happened to Tabitha's expression. She looked startled, then smug. "Actually, I just left her in the cafeteria."

"What's she doing in the cafeteria? Her shift starts—" he looked at his watch "—five minutes ago."

"She came in early to check on a girl who got admitted last night. A domestic-violence situation."

"Oh, man." Sam grimaced. He hated those.

"One of the police detectives—Molly Gates—notified her," Tabitha explained. "The girl's the sister of a boy we treated several months ago—he was a victim of those crooked cops, that 'Lion's Den' thing. Apparently Detective Gates has a soft spot for the family, and she wanted someone she trusted to look in on the child.''

Bobby Jansen. Sam remembered. ''His sister's here now? What happened?''

Tabitha looked miserable. ''A run-in with her mother's boyfriend. Anyway, Cait's been with Beatty since early this morning and she just ran downstairs for a cup of tea before her shift officially starts.''

''Thanks.'' Sam strode down the hallway toward the elevator.

Tea? What kind of woman drank tea? he thought. The kind who drove microscopic, sensible cars, he answered himself. The kind who could dance with a glass of champagne in her hand. The kind with big, blue, innocent eyes that told a whole lot of different stories, depending on the day and her mood.

Sam put the Jansen girl out of his mind for the time being. First, there was a certain nurse he needed to get out of his system.

He found her in the cafeteria, just as Tabitha had said. She was cleaning up her table as though the Board of Health was expected to pour into the room at any given moment. She wiped it down with her napkin, then she folded that into little quarters before she dropped it into the trash bin. This, Sam thought, was the woman who had always irritated the hell out of him.

When she glanced up, he saw something happen to her eyes. They went wide, and he swore he saw heat there before they thinned. She crossed to him resolutely.

''I'm on my way upstairs now,'' she said when she reached him.

"No hurry." He crossed his arms over his chest, going for the casual and laid-back look. Like a friend, he thought—and one-time lover—instead of a co-worker.

"What's this?" she asked suspiciously.

"What's what?"

"This." She mimicked his stance.

Sam dropped his arms. "It's nothing. I just wanted to talk to you."

"You could have caught me upstairs in two minutes." When he hesitated, she sighed. "Sam, my reasons for wanting a transfer are still personal."

"'Sam,'" he repeated, leaning a little closer to her. "You know, you do have a way of saying that."

He saw something pink touch her neck before she stepped back quickly. "Well, you won't have to listen to it much longer."

"Cait, I really don't want to lose you."

She took another step in retreat. "You never had me."

He lowered his voice. "I did. Once. And I liked it."

This time heat definitely flared in her eyes. But just as quickly, it was gone again. "That—as well as our professional relationship—is over now," she said. She started to move around him.

Sam had to sidestep fast to block her way. "I have an idea. Let me take you out for dinner tonight and we can discuss this transfer business in more detail."

"Dinner?" Her voice sounded like a squeak.

"Two people in a restaurant sharing wine and good food and conversation," he clarified.

"Ask Dr. Leon." She tried to bolt past him. He moved again.

"Dr. Leon and I no longer have unfinished business."

"Then excuse me for a moment while I call in the drum-and-bugle corps."

She was doing it again, he thought. She was being sarcastic. He had to fight hard not to laugh. "On the other hand," he said, "you and I do."

"Not really. My transfer goes through on Wednesday." She inched to her left, still trying to get around him. "I just found out this morning. Elizabeth Halverson in neonatal is willing to trade positions with me. You'll like her."

"Not as much as I like you."

Cait stumbled. "Stop this! Stop it right now!"

"I will if you'll agree to have dinner with me and talk this over."

Her eyes narrowed. "Why would you want to keep me? Since I've been back you've jumped on every little move I've made."

"Trust me, it's had nothing to do with your work ethic."

Wrong words, he thought immediately. He saw her stiffen.

"Don't you dare let one affect the other!" she said hotly. "What happened between us in that room was a mistake. We both admitted it. I want to move on now. If you dare use it to influence my career—"

"I didn't say that!" he almost shouted, exasperated.

She sniffed. "You implied it."

"The hell I did!"

"You mentioned my work ethic."

"I *like* your work ethic. That's what I said." How had she turned this all around?

"Okay, then."

Sam frowned. "Okay?"

"That's what I said. Okay. Can I go now?"

"What about dinner?"

"I'm sure Dr. Leon will enjoy it very much."

She was, he realized, talking circles around him. "I just told you, it's over with her."

"Then find a new trophy, Sam. But it's not going to be me." This time she managed to duck past him.

Sam gaped after her as one of the cafeteria workers came to pull the plastic bag out of the trash bin near where they had been standing. "Uh-oh," the woman said. "What was that all about? It sounded like a lovers' spat. Is she your girlfriend?"

It was kind of a personal question for a stranger to be asking, Sam thought. He looked at the woman and tried to figure out if he knew her. She had short brown hair and murky blue eyes, the kind of hue that resulted when someone with dark eyes tried to lighten them with tinted lenses. She was slightly overweight, but her uniform was still too large as though she was trying to camouflage unwanted swells and curves. It was Sam's firm opinion that women often went overboard in trying to correct what they saw as weaknesses, and that was a shame.

"She's not my girlfriend," he said absently. "She's my, uh..." He trailed off. His mind went blank for a moment. "Nemesis."

"Well, good for her," said a familiar voice behind him.

Sam jerked around. "Nancy."

"Interesting scene," she said, looking past him at the door Cait had escaped through.

"That wasn't a scene."

"You know, you're starting to sound like a man who's seriously in denial."

Sam scowled darkly as he looked at the door again, too.

"I especially liked the part where she imitated you." Nancy crossed her arms over her chest the way Cait had. "Whoever would have guessed the little mouse had it in her?"

"She's not a mouse." He heard the edge to his voice and winced. Where had *that* come from?

"Are you actually sticking up for her?" Nancy asked.

Sam let out a rough breath. "I don't think she needs it."

"Me, neither," Nancy said, sweeping past him. Then she paused and turned back, poking a finger into his chest. "You, my dear, have finally met your match."

When she was gone, Sam stood for a long time rubbing a hand against the sore spot she'd left. Nancy's fingernails had always been dangerous.

His match? Five foot two inches of starch? "I'm getting her out of my system, damn it." Or he would have been well on his way, he thought, if she'd just agreed to have dinner with him.

Now what was he supposed to do?

By the time she returned to the cafeteria at lunchtime, Cait was reasonably sure it was going to be the longest day of her life. Her nerves felt like the most fragile porcelain. If Sam had been rude and antagonistic toward her before, today he was going out of his way to be chivalrous. She knew what he was up to, of course. He was trying to get her to change her mind about the transfer. Which still made no sense, she thought desperately. He ought to be glad that she was so effectively putting the whole business of what had happened between them behind her.

That was what he'd said he wanted.

Cait wasn't sure which was worse—his charm or his irritation. She felt as though she was on an emotional roller coaster. His kindness, his jokes, made something melt inside her.

She nibbled halfway through an egg-salad sandwich before she realized that her stomach was a little off again. She pushed her plate away and started to get up for another cup of tea when Nancy Walters dropped into the chair across from her, groaning a little.

"One thing I liked about living off Sam's alimony," the woman said, "was that I didn't have to wear heels." She toed off one of her shoes and rubbed her instep. "My feet are killing me."

Cait felt anger spike in her. She had the insane urge to tell the woman that she ought to go confide in someone who cared. Instead, she sank back into her chair. "Then why did you get a job?" she asked politely.

Nancy sighed. "Sheer boredom. Plus, I thought I'd get out a little and meet a man on my own terms rather than suffer the blind dates my father lines up for me these days. He's determined to see me married again." She shrugged. "I'm only here part time."

"That's nice." Cait nodded stiffly.

"You're annoyed with me, aren't you?"

"Of course not." Then Cait hesitated. Whether it was PTSD or hormones, she really was tired of being nice all the time. The fact remained that it had gotten her nowhere. "Yes," she amended.

Nancy looked startled, then she laughed. "Fair enough. But you have no cause. I didn't tell Sam anything."

"Except where I live."

"No, I didn't."

Cait shrugged and stood again. "It doesn't matter. I have to get back to work."

"He does seem pretty upset about losing you, though," Nancy said as though Cait hadn't spoken.

"He'll get over it." Cait picked up her plate. Her stomach no longer even felt up to tea.

"All I'm saying is that I probably know him better than any other woman on earth," Nancy continued. "If you want a sounding board, I'm available."

Cait looked at her quickly. "So you can run to him with every word I say?"

The woman held up one hand in a pledge. "I won't. Scout's honor. But something clearly very personal is going on between you two."

"No, it's not!" Cait heard her voice rise before she got a grip on herself. "Thanks for your concern, but I'm fine."

She left Nancy and went to scrape her plate into the trash can, then took it back to the counter. She had one more thing to do on her lunch break: make an appointment with an obstetrician in Laredo. She had a whole pocketful of change for the toll call. She'd already decided that while she was in the city, she would put out a few job applications and look at apartments.

"Is everything all right?" asked the woman behind the counter as she took her plate.

Cait focused on her. Her thoughts were miles away on a new city where she really would be utterly alone. She'd miss Tabitha, she realized with a pang.

And Sam. But she couldn't think about Sam.

"You look upset," the woman observed.

Cait shook her head. "I'm not." Then she hesitated. "Do I know you?"

"Only from in here. I'm Holly Sinclair."

"Oh. Well, nice to meet you." Cait turned away.

"I noticed you arguing with Dr. Walters earlier this morning," Holly said.

Cait glanced back at her. "I work with him. We were just having a disagreement about a patient." She heard the lie slide from her tongue as effortlessly as so many others had lately and she cringed inwardly. What was happening to her? But her shame wasn't enough to topple her disquiet over all these people suddenly poking into her business.

She shuddered visibly and hurried out of the cafeteria. The sooner she made a clean break from this place, the better.

Well, the woman thought, that hadn't been very enlightening. She watched Cait flee the cafeteria for the second time that day and glanced at her watch.

It was just past noon. The nurse would be on duty for a while yet. That left her time.

"If at first you don't succeed," the woman murmured aloud, "try again. None of this would be necessary if she wasn't such an unfriendly little snob."

She gave Cait a decent head start, then followed her out of the cafeteria. It was time for Plan B. She headed up the hallway and slipped into the personnel office—it was deserted because everyone was on break. She went to the big, blue metal filing cabinet that held the records of every employee in the hospital. She had, of course, taken a leisurely stroll through many of them before.

She found the one for Caitlyn Matthews and checked for her address and her schedule. A copy of her transfer request was in there, as well, and the woman smiled at that. Cait Matthews might just solve the problem herself when that transfer went through. But she still wanted to know what had sent her flying out of the ball the other night.

Cait worked the eight-to-four shift. The woman had known that, of course, but she needed to make absolutely sure. She put the file back and sauntered out again, returning to the cafeteria.

Her adrenaline built consistently over the next couple of hours. By two o'clock, it was something alive in her blood, hot and sweet, singing. She left the hospital and drove to Cait's address on Euclid Street.

At first she was startled. The home there was large and white, somewhat ramshackle but pretty. The drive and walkway were lined with an incredible snarl of flowers in so many colors it hurt the eyes. Nurse Perfect obviously had some money stashed away to be able to afford this, she thought, and that only made her hate her more.

Then she noticed that the driveway led back to a garage, and that there were curtains on the windows of the second floor there. Cait probably lived back there. That made more sense, the woman thought, but it was a complication. Someone obviously lived in the house in the front and they might even be home, might notice her approaching the apartment in the back. She could always pretend to be a friend of Cait's, but still, it would raise a few eyebrows when she had to break into the place....

The woman drove a little farther up the street and parked there to think the problem out.

It was only by sheer luck that she happened to glance into her rearview mirror at the exact time a pale-yellow behemoth of an automobile lumbered out of the drive. An ancient woman with hair in tight white curls was driving. As she inched the car past at a cautious crawl, she hunched forward to grip the steering wheel in both gnarly white hands.

"Good enough," the watcher said aloud. Now she was willing to take her chances. She got out of the car and forced herself not to hurry as she went back to the driveway.

An equally old male geezer might still be in residence in the big white house, she thought, but judging by the looks of his wife, his sight and hearing could be counted on to be imperfect. She headed up the drive as though she belonged there. The garage door was up now. The old woman hadn't bothered to lower it. Was there a way to the upstairs apartment from inside?

The woman stepped into the garage and peered around, noticing stairs in the back. She climbed them, then tried the knob on the door at the top.

Locked up tight. Picturing Cait Matthews, she wasn't surprised.

But the lock was one of those silly, old-fashioned types right in the handle, she discovered, the kind that a five-year-old could get through. The woman ran one long, painted fingernail back and forth in the narrow space between the door and the jam, trying to catch the bolt.

Close, but not quite. She went back downstairs again and sorted through a pile of odds and ends on an old workbench.

Everything was coated with dust. If the old lady had a husband who had once used this stuff, then he was either incapacitated now or dead. No one had touched any of these tools in a very long time. She found an awl, better for her purposes than anything she might have hoped for. She went back upstairs and used it to remove the doorknob entirely.

She stepped into a kitchen so tidy it offended her. She stopped and sniffed at pristine air. Maybe, she thought, there was a hint of garlic in it, but if so, the prissy nurse had all but banished its source with air freshener and a good dose of detergent. The stove and counters gleamed in the sunlight that slanted through the single kitchen window.

The woman drove her fingers into her hair while she looked around, frowning. She wasn't sure what she was looking for, but she knew she'd recognize it when she saw it.

She finally moved into the living room, cramped

and small and dark now because the sun was hitting the back of the garage and this room looked out on the street. There were antiques everywhere—washbasins and lamps and doodads, even a red leather chair that looked interesting. The woman picked up a brass candle snuffer and inspected it, then the hairs at her nape lifted.

"Yeowl!"

She cried out and jumped at the sound. The snuffer went flying from her hand to land against one wooden arm of the leather chair with a crack. The bell snapped cleanly off.

"Jeez!" Her heart was bucking. She looked around as she clapped a hand to her chest. A large orange cat sat in the threshold to what was probably a bedroom. "You scared the hell out of me!"

The beast opened his mouth and hissed.

"Oh, shut up. Look what you did." The woman crossed the room to retrieve the candle snuffer. She fussed with it for a moment, but there was no putting it back together. She replaced it on the crowded sideboard where she'd found it, balancing the handle on top of the bell just so. The twit would never even know it was broken unless she picked it up, and why would she? There wasn't a single candle in the room. Although, knowing Nurse Matthews, she probably dusted everything in this jumbled place before she slept each night.

The woman headed for the bedroom. That was where secrets were usually kept. The cat didn't move.

"Shoo." She waved a hand at him. He wouldn't leave the doorway. She tried to step over him and he gave a rumbling, growling sound of warning. "Okay, we'll do this the hard way.'' She reached down and grabbed him by the scruff of the neck. She'd known a cat or two in her time. They always went docile in such a grip. It was the way their mothers held them when they were kittens.

This one went insane.

He curled his whole fat body into a ball, legs flailing, claws slashing as he tried to reach her with one of them. He twisted, angling his head even in spite of her grip, flashing teeth at her, trying to bite her. The woman swore, holding him as far away from herself as possible. He was heavy. She was going to lose her hold on him. If he got loose, then what would he do to her?

She ran back to the kitchen with him and made it to the door there, the one that led downstairs into the garage. The cat's back claws raked her forearm. She bit back another curse and tossed him out on the steps, then quickly closed the door.

After a few moments of silence, she dared to open the door a crack to peer through. She didn't see any sign of the cat in the gloom on the other side. She closed the door again and began to move back across the kitchen when she noticed that she was dripping blood on the floor.

''Damn, damn, damn.'' She thought of DNA and then snorted. Nobody tested for DNA over for a simple breaking-and-entering—and that was assuming Cait even called the cops in the first place. She probably would never even realize that anyone had been in her home. Still, there was the broken candle snuffer.

The woman ripped a paper towel off the roll and

wiped up the blood, then wrapped it around her wrist to staunch the flow once the floor was clean. Then she took another towel and went to wipe the candle snuffer free of her fingerprints, as well. She pocketed both paper towels and finally made it into the bedroom.

A single bed? What kind of woman slept in a single bed? Dumb question, she answered herself, then she began to poke through Cait's dresser drawers. She found not a single thing worth mentioning until she happened to look down as she stepped into the bathroom. Her gaze landed on the trash can there and her eyes bugged.

What was that? A *pregnancy* test?

The woman stared at it, then threw back her head and laughed, delighted. She had to hold her stomach when the spasms kept coming and started to hurt. Finally she hunkered down beside the can and reached in for the little stick.

She'd taken a number of these tests herself, praying through the whole course of her marriage that she'd conceive. She knew what she was looking at. It was exactly what she had longed to see on little sticks like this too many times to count.

The bitch was pregnant.

Suddenly, rage exploded in her head and tears stung at her eyes. She dropped the stick back into the trash and shot to her feet. She looked around the pretty blue-and-white room, wanting to smash it, to destroy everything she saw. No, no, no. She mustn't do that. She pressed her hands to the sides of her head, instead, against the pain rocking through her skull.

At least now she knew what had gone on in that basement room between Sam Walters and Cait Matthews. No wonder they had been so chummy in that storage room.

She forced herself to breathe evenly, deeply, getting her control back. She told herself that this was actually a boon. It was definitely something she could use. She just wasn't sure how yet.

She left the bedroom, shaken to her core. On the way out, she inspected everything, trying to remember what all she had touched. The scratch on her arm was starting to sting now. Finally she was satisfied that everything looked the way it had when she had come in.

It took her five more minutes to put the doorknob back in place. Then she waited at the foot of the stairs for a moment, listening to make sure the old lady wasn't coming back.

There was no car coming. She walked calmly out of the garage. Once she got halfway down the drive, she knew she was home free. If the old woman came back now, she could simply say she'd been looking for Cait, but no one had answered her knock on the apartment door. Of course, the old woman would know what she looked like then, would be able to identify her, but that would only matter if Cait ever realized someone had been in her apartment and called the police. That, the woman thought again, really wasn't likely.

She went back to her car and drove home, her mind racing, wondering what to do now.

Seven

Cait dragged herself up the outside stairs to her apartment at half-past four, feeling as though her shoes were made of lead. It was part of being pregnant, she thought, actually cherishing it. She was already starting to experience that overriding tiredness as her body got the hint that another human being was growing inside her.

There was a feeling of satisfaction in her chest, too, and she smiled as she started fitting her keys into the locks on her door. Things were starting to come together. She'd made an appointment with an obstetrician in Laredo—a name picked out of the medical directory behind the nurses' station—but she could always change later if she decided she didn't like the man. She'd withstood Sam's charm all day without budging an inch. In fact, she'd managed to antagonize him.

It would be so much easier to leave him behind if she'd never learned to cherish his grins, his charm, his humor. But in just two more days she'd be safely tucked away in the neonatal unit, well away from him. She only had to remain strong against him for another shift.

She wasn't sure she had it in her.

Cait stepped into her apartment and dropped her

purse on the chair near the door. "See, right on schedule this time," she said to Billy. "You don't have a thing to worry about."

She headed for the window to gather him up and pet him, then she frowned and paused. The cat wasn't on the window ledge.

"Billy?" She pivoted in place, looking around the room. "Here, kitty, kitty." Her heart lurched. He must be sick. It was the only reason she could think of that he wouldn't be in the window watching for her.

She hurried into the bedroom but he wasn't there, either. She got to her knees and peered under the bed. Nothing. Her pulse accelerated as she stuck her head into the bathroom. She came up empty there, too.

"Billy," she said. "What's wrong? Where are you?"

She went back to the living room. Until that moment she had never realized how much she had come to depend on his company since she'd rescued him from the pound. How much she needed him. Where could he have gone?

She should never have let herself love anything again, she thought helplessly, never. She pressed her fingers to her temples as though it would help her think, then began ripping the pillows from the sofa, feeling terrified and foolish both at once. She dropped to the floor to look under the sofa, too. The last sensible thing in her head told her to be absolutely sure that the cat was gone before she became unglued.

She looked under the chair and in the coat closet. She yanked open the drawers of the sideboard, as though a fat, old orange tabby could somehow manage to squeeze his way inside one. She laughed shrilly at herself and slammed them shut again. The stem of the candle snuffer on top fell off its little bell.

Cait went utterly still and stared at it.

Finally, with a shaking hand, she reached and picked it up. She used her other hand to scrub at the back of her neck. *Someone was watching her again.*

"No, no, no," she whispered. She was at home. She was alone. No one was here. She'd just been through the entire apartment. No one's eyes were on her.

She went to the window and looked out, anyway. No one was there.

But someone had *been* here. Her candle snuffer was broken and Billy was gone.

She finally realized that the keening sound filling the air was coming from her own throat. She dropped the snuffer stem to the carpet and pressed her hand to her mouth. It wasn't the PTSD and it wasn't pregnancy hormones making her nuts, she realized. Someone was after her. Someone really *had* been watching her, following her.

A twelve-pound tabby didn't let himself out of a locked apartment by himself, and candle snuffers didn't fall apart on their own.

Terror speared through her, robbing her of breath. This was every bit as mind-numbing as when Hines had finally shoved her forward into the laundry chute that day when she'd started making her way toward it too slowly. Cait sank to the floor and curled herself into a little ball, finally crying.

* * *

There was always more than one way to skin a cat, Sam thought, letting himself into his condo at a quarter past five. He just had to figure out what they were.

Houdini barked in greeting and Sam scratched him absently between the ears, shedding his tie on his way to the answering machine. A big red goose egg stared back at him from the number-of-calls window. No calls. That was bad. Really bad.

He had to get a handle on this situation before it spiraled totally out of control. He had to convince Cait to see him again.

Again? He laughed hoarsely and scrubbed a hand over his mouth. Their first encounter had hardly been a matter of *seeing* each other. A madman had grabbed them and stuck them in a cement room. They'd…reacted. They'd reached out for each other.

Sam knew honestly that he would never have asked Cait out had that not happened. Of course, if that hadn't happened, he'd never have known about the spitfire lurking underneath those starched scrubs of hers.

Now she had his attention, and he wanted to see her. Socially, intimately, whatever. Just to get her off his mind, he reminded himself. Except, for the first time in his memory, a woman wanted nothing to do with him.

It occurred to Sam that he'd barely thought of anything but her all day, puzzling at the situation, worrying over it, becoming more and more irritated by it. Between patients, he'd watched her. He'd never once caught her watching him back.

Three weeks ago he would have said she was ice to the bone. But he knew better now. So the only explanation was that she was *trying* to drive him crazy.

Maybe she was playing hard to get. Sam snapped his fingers. That was it. Except…he'd asked her out and she had refused him. Women played hard to get in order to snag a man's interest. He'd given her his—and she'd tossed it right back in his face again.

Houdini barked one more time.

"Will you be quiet?" Sam snapped. "I'm trying to think here." He went to the kitchen for a beer. The retriever followed him.

"You're not going out running," he told him, grabbing a bottle out of the refrigerator. "You've already used up your allowance for the week. I'm not dropping another twenty-five bucks on you before Friday."

Houdini made a rumbling sound in his throat. Suddenly Sam stopped in midmotion as he began to unscrew the cap from the bottle. He stared at the dog as something occurred to him. "Good thinking."

The dog's tongue hung out. He seemed to be grinning.

Sam put the unopened bottle back in the refrigerator. It took three minutes for him to put on gym shorts and hunt down his running shoes. But then he took off the shorts, deciding he needed a quick shower. After that he stepped into jeans and pulled on a polo shirt, hitting the bathroom one more time to brush his teeth. Then he stopped back in the bedroom to slap on some cologne.

Finally he went to find the dog's leash. Cait wanted him. Of course, she wanted him. She'd made love with him, no matter what the circumstances.

That said something loud and clear. She was probably just worried about his less-than-conventional tendencies, he decided. She knew better than to get involved with a man who defied order in nearly every aspect of his life except professionally.

Of course, he wasn't talking about getting involved with her. Not really. He just wanted to spend a little more time with her so they could both come to the conclusion that they were all wrong for each other. But first, to do that, he had to get past her barriers so she'd go out with him. He had to be a little more...well, conventional.

So he would walk his dog, instead of turning him loose in the pet area. And if he happened to end up on Euclid Street, well, all the better.

He snapped on Houdini's leash and they went downstairs. Then, in the parking lot, Sam hesitated. Euclid Street was a good mile away. He was too impatient to take the time to walk.

"Come on, pal. We're going sightseeing." He led the dog to his car, unlocked it and let the big beast jump up into the passenger seat. "Scratch that leather with your monster toenails and you die."

The dog shot him a look as if to say that clippers were his master's responsibility. Sam ignored him and went around to the other side of the car, getting behind the wheel.

He drove to within four blocks of Cait's apartment. Then he parked, leashed the dog, and they proceeded the rest of the way on foot. "This," he told Houdini when they were a block away, "is how conventional guys do this."

In response, the dog gave a blood-throbbing howl and lunged forward.

Sam actually took several running steps with the absurd idea of either keeping up with him or controlling him again. Then Houdini gave another ferocious yank on the leash, and Sam thought his arm might come out of the socket. He let go of the leather in self-defense, swearing, rubbing his shoulder.

Houdini was off and running. But he didn't go far. As Sam watched, he cut into a driveway a block ahead. And unless Sam badly missed his guess, it was Cait's driveway.

"Damned dog can't be that smart," he muttered. "Can he?" Then he broke into a jog to go after him.

By the time he got to the driveway, the din was incredible. It was most definitely Cait's address. The retriever was howling and pacing around a tree in the small yard between the white house and the garage where Cait lived. Houdini stopped periodically to jump up and brace his paws on the trunk, barking for all he was worth.

In response, the tree yowled.

Not the tree, Sam realized, running that way. The cat. Cait had a cat. A big, orange thing that had had a pretty tough life these past few weeks. Tabitha Monroe had taken it into her head to use him to meet Hines's ransom demands when he and Cait had been held hostage in his underground room.

This, he thought, was good. He could rescue the cat. Cait would be grateful and with any luck, her good manners would necessitate she repay him by having dinner with him. Sam reached the tree and sidestepped Houdini, looking for a handhold on a branch so he could climb up.

Then he heard a shriek.

Sam's gaze shot to the garage and he saw Cait coming down the steps at such a clip his heart froze. "Be careful! You're going to—" He broke off as she reached the fourth step from the bottom and simply leaped the rest, landing on the driveway like some sort of trapeze artist, fluidly and without missing stride.

She kept coming straight at him. And she was shouting. Sam took a cautious step backward. "What—"

He never got the question out. She hit him in the chest with both hands. "What have you done?" she demanded.

"Me? I was just getting—"

She beat her fists against his chest. "No more! Do you understand me? *No more!* I'm not going to let you unravel my life!"

"I was getting your cat!"

"He wouldn't even be out here in the first place except for you and Hines and…and…"

"Are you accusing me of letting your cat out?" He was dumbfounded at the turn this encounter had taken.

"I'm accusing you of getting me evicted!"

"Over a cat?"

"Over *that!*" she shouted, pointing at the dog.

"What's that dog doing here?" called an old woman from the back porch of the house.

"I don't know," Cait called back.

"Treeing the cat," Sam said reasonably.

"Are you the man who came here the other day in that noisy car?" the woman asked.

"Probably," Sam said. He looked at Cait. "Is she talking about me? What does Estrada drive?"

She looked at him as though he had lost his mind, then she launched into him with her fists all over again. It wasn't until he'd caught her wrists to protect himself that Sam really got a look at her face.

She was crying.

Sam felt his breath stall. His heart tightened into a hard little knot that hurt. "Hey, hey, what's all this about?" he asked quietly.

Cait felt suddenly mortified, and his concern stoked something inside her. She yanked away from him and turned her back, digging the heels of her hands into her eyes to dry them. She would not fall apart in front of him.

She already had, she thought. She was being totally, completely irrational.

"It's about your dog." She sniffed. "Make him go."

"How do you know it's my dog?" he asked evasively.

She glanced back at him disbelievingly.

"Okay, okay, he's my dog." He held out his hands as though to placate her. "Just hold on, okay? Don't leave yet."

"I'm not going back inside without my cat."

"Good, because I want to talk to you." Sam turned to the tree again and wrapped both arms around Houdini's neck to restrain him. "Can you get me a rope?"

"What for?"

"So I can tie him up."

"Why?"

"So I can find out why you're crying without worrying about him taking off. I'm a very conventional dog owner."

Cait looked at him oddly, then scrubbed her hands over her cheeks. "I'm fine. Get your dog and go home."

"What about your cat?"

"I'll lure him down after you're gone." Cait glanced at the house. Mrs. Brody was still watching. Her heart squeezed. "It'll just be another moment," she assured the old woman as the golden retriever started howling again.

"I have a rope," the woman offered.

"Thanks, I'd appreciate that," Sam said.

"That's not necessary," Cait said quickly. "He's not staying."

But Mrs. Brody scurried inside and came back with a rope. She hustled to the yard with her little bird steps and handed it to Sam. He used it to lash the dog to the tree. The horrible animal kept barking.

"Will he stay put now?" Mrs. Brody asked worriedly.

"Probably not for long," Sam said. Then he climbed the tree and came down with the cat, who was hissing and clawing madly. He shoved Billy into Cait's arms.

The cat was the best thing she had felt all day. Cait buried her face in his fur as he calmed down a little. "Thanks," she whispered. "You can go now."

"Not without antiseptic."

She looked at him quickly, her insides shaking. "What?"

He held up his scratched hands in response. Cait winced. "I'm sorry." Then her mind reeled. She was sorry? His dog had started all this! "What kind of an idiot would own something like that incorrigible mutt, anyway?"

"He's not a mutt. He's a purebred." Sam's eyes narrowed. "Are you casting aspersions on my dog?"

"Yes. He's crazed!"

"He's a dog. Dogs chase cats. It's in their blood. What kind of a sparrow would own a cat?"

Cait felt her spine snap straight. "Cats are mannerly, neat, quiet." She glanced pointedly at the dog, who was still barking. She shuddered at the mere thought of the chaos involved with owning one, then she noticed Mrs. Brody watching them avidly.

Sam wasn't going to leave easily, she thought. And she wasn't about to argue with him in front of her landlady, either. Mrs. Brody was—God forbid— probably getting ready to serve her with eviction papers right then and there. Cait freed one hand from Billy and grabbed Sam's arm. "Come on."

"Where are we going?" he asked warily.

"I'm going to clean those scratches for you. I'm a nurse, remember?"

"And a very good one," he assured her.

She glared at him. "Stuff it."

"That was a compliment," he said indignantly as they climbed the steps.

Now that she was sure he would come with her, Cait dropped his arm. She couldn't touch him, not even casually. It made something curl too deliciously in the pit of her stomach. ''It wasn't a compliment. You were kissing up to me. Though for the life of me, I can't figure out why.''

''I've explained that already.''

She ignored that. ''Wait for me right there.'' They stepped over the threshold into her apartment and she pointed at the kitchen.

''My mother always used to fix me up in the bathroom,'' Sam said.

''I'm not your mother.'' And the only way to get to her bathroom was through her bedroom. Cait felt something shiver inside her at the thought of letting him get that close to the heart of her. Though he'd already gotten pretty close. So close, in fact, that...

She pressed a hand to her stomach with the thought, then steeled herself and stalked off.

She put Billy on the bed and took a moment to rub him between the ears. ''Poor baby.'' His hair was still all puffed up from his encounter with the dog. She went into the bathroom and found a bottle of hydrogen peroxide. For what she had in mind, it was all she needed.

Cait went back to the living room and found Sam still standing there. ''What are you doing?'' she asked as he looked around.

''Trying to figure out what makes you tick.''

Something about his tone told her he was serious. Her heart shifted. ''It doesn't matter.''

''Under the circumstances, I think it does.''

He was talking as if he knew about the baby. Her heart slugged. But that was impossible. ''My living room isn't going to impart any clues.''

He finally looked at her. "It already has. You like old things."

She glanced around at her almost-antiques and flushed. "They're not that old."

"Things with character," he clarified. "Things that last."

Like nothing else in her life ever had, Cait thought. But this baby would. This child would be with her forever.

Suddenly she ached with the need to make him understand why she needed to get away from him, why he needed to leave her alone so she could love this baby in peace. The urge to talk, to spill things out, was so strong she turned away into the kitchen, shaken by it. "Do you want me to clean those scratches, or are you just going to let them fester?"

He followed her, eyeing the bottle of peroxide. "You're going to hurt me."

"Yes. And I'm looking forward to it. Hold your hands over the sink."

He did and she saw him tighten his jaw, bracing himself for it. "What did I ever do to you?" he muttered.

You made me want something I can't have. "Your dog terrorized my cat." She splashed the peroxide over his hands.

He yelled as it foamed up on the scratches. "Jeez! Ever hear of cotton swabs?"

"I don't have any."

"I'll bet. You've probably got clamps on the off chance you have to perform open-heart surgery on your kitchen table."

"Are you calling me rigid again?"

"Have dinner with me and prove to me that you're not."

She'd already proved it once, Cait thought, and it had gotten her…here. Pregnant, which was overwhelming and wonderful. With Sam seeming as though he wanted to set his sights on her, which was confusing and terrifyingly enticing.

Her hands were a little unsteady as she screwed the cap back on the bottle. "I can't."

"Why not?"

I'm pregnant with your child. Cait put the peroxide bottle down and pressed her palms to her cheeks. It was like an alien being had taken up residence in her mind, hissing words that she didn't dare speak aloud. And with the way she'd been acting lately, any one of them was liable to come out for real.

"Cait?" he said. "What's wrong?"

She dropped her hands and glared at him. "You're in my kitchen, that's what's wrong."

"You know, it just occurs to me that you're being a lot more antagonistic toward me than the situation between us warrants."

"There's no situation between us," she whispered desperately.

"Not if you won't let there be one. I'm trying to convince you otherwise."

She shook her head hard and fast as she thought of Billy and the candle snuffer again. "I have enough on my mind without…without…"

Sam watched, waiting for her to finish. But she only moved one hand to press it against her mouth, then she turned away. This time he noticed that the hand was shaking and her eyes went bright as though she was going to cry again.

Something inside him hurt to see her this way. She was the steadiest, kindest, calmest woman he had ever met—even when Hines had been in the process of abducting them. So what was this? "Look at me," he said quietly.

"No." Her voice came back muffled. "If you don't leave now, I'll…I'll call the police and have you removed."

"Oh, sure. Your landlady would love that kind of commotion."

She turned back to face him, and her eyes shot fire. "This is none of your concern. It's me this time, just me. Not you."

Finally it hit him.

The way she'd run out of the apartment down the stairs when Houdini had gone after the cat. She'd already been crying. She'd already been wild. "Something's happened to you," he said. His voice was flat, implacable, something he rarely heard from himself. And whatever it was had happened before he'd even arrived. It had nothing to do with Houdini.

He watched her look around the kitchen as though seeking an answer. He still didn't think she'd give him one, but then she surprised him. She sat down suddenly at the kitchen table as though someone had removed the bones from her legs, groping a little for the chair and easing herself into it. "Someone broke in here," she said in a voice so small he almost didn't hear it.

But the words hit him like sledgehammers. "When?" he asked harshly.

"Today. Billy was here when I left for work this morning," she said desperately.

"What does the cat have to do with it?"

She looked up at him, something in her eyes flaring again. "Because he was here, then he wasn't! When I got home, he was gone! That means someone put him outside!"

"Maybe he scooted out the door when you left this morning." He wanted desperately for there to be a reasonable explanation for this. Because if there wasn't, then someone was still after her.

Cait shot to her feet again. "Billy has no urge to go outside," she said. "He doesn't like it outside. I've owned him for years, and he's never once made a dash for the door." She paused, then added, "They broke my candle snuffer, too."

"Your what?"

"This." She headed into the living room and he followed her. She picked it up from the floor where she'd dropped it earlier.

"How do you know it wasn't broken before?" he asked.

"Because I don't break things!"

There was that, he thought. "Okay. Where's your phone?"

"Why?"

"I'm going to do something about this."

"Whoever was here didn't leave a calling card."

"I'm calling the police, damn it!"

"Why are you yelling at me?"

"Because I can't stand you being scared. It does something to me."

Everything inside her went still, then shimmered.

No, no, don't let that happen. Don't let him get to you. But she wished it was true. It made something achy bloom inside her.

She couldn't quite find her voice.

He went to look for a phone without her telling him where to find it. It took Cait several moments to go after him. He'd located the kitchen extension and was hanging up when she got there.

"They're on their way," he said.

"But what can they possibly do?" she asked shakily.

"For one thing, they can tell us where Branson Hines is."

Her face bleached. She felt it happen, felt the blood drain to her toes. "He's in jail. And why me? Even if he got free again, why come after *me?* I was just someone in the wrong place at the wrong time that day. I never met him before in my life. He can't possibly have a grudge against me."

Sam shook his head. "I don't know. Maybe he's just ticked off that we escaped."

"Then he'd go after you, too! Has anything weird happened to you?"

Sam thought about it. "No." Not unless he counted the way she was getting to him.

The police arrived in record time. Cait heard the cruiser pull up outside before she even had a chance to clear her head so she could face them. She wasn't sure if she was comforted by their arrival or embarrassed about the way they'd come so quickly. She went to the door to let them in.

They were a man-and-woman team. The woman was pretty and freckled and brusque. The man was young with dewy brown eyes and a quiet voice. Sam trailed after the woman as she began to inspect the apartment. The man motioned at Cait to sit on the sofa.

She did so obediently. He sat beside her. "I'm Officer Nodesky," he said.

"It's a pleasure to meet you." Cait giggled a little nervously at her response. Polite to the death, she thought shakily. "Thanks for coming."

He grinned, setting her at ease. Cait spent the next ten minutes outlining how she knew someone had been in the apartment. Was that skepticism she saw in his eyes? Did he think she was strung out, crazy, because of her kidnapping ordeal? He'd be right, she thought desperately, except she was absolutely sure that someone had been here. Cait opened her mouth to tell him about the feeling lately that she was being watched, then Sam and the other officer came back into the room.

"When was the last time you changed that door-knob in the kitchen?" the woman asked. Her name tag read L. Needles, Cait saw.

She frowned. "Changed it?"

"Took it off and replaced it?"

"Never," Cait said. "I've never done that. Why would I?"

L. Needles scribbled something in her notepad and looked at her partner. "That's how they came in," she told him. "There are fresh scratch marks on it and it's wiped clean. My guess is that the scratches are from a tool of some kind. One of the work-benches downstairs in the garage has been disturbed. There's dust all over everything except that."

Officer Nodesky looked at Cait. "Is anything missing? Did you notice anything else amiss besides the candle snuffer and your pet?"

Cait flushed. "I really didn't look. I didn't have a chance." She looked accusingly at Sam. "His dog caused a scene, then he called you and you came right away."

"Does your landlord live in the house?" Nodesky asked.

Cait nodded woodenly. "Landlady," she corrected. "Her name is Mrs. Brody."

"I'll go talk to her."

As soon as he was gone, Sam took his place on the sofa. Cait looked at him warily. But in the end, when he took her hand and stroked a thumb over her knuckles, she let him. It sent little shivers and shock waves through her system, but she let him.

It felt so good not to be alone right now.

"You've got to know that Branson Hines comes to our mind at a time like this," Sam said to Officer Needles.

Cait gripped his hand hard and nodded her agreement.

"That's understandable," the officer said. "But he's in jail."

"You're sure about that? He escaped once before."

"Not this time. I had the desk sergeant make a phone call while my partner and I drove over here. Hines is present and accounted for in his cell."

"What about his wife?"

"She's in Laredo. She left town right after he was

taken into custody and he's been making repeated phone calls from the jail to a fleabag motel there.''

''That's that, then,'' Cait said. But it made no sense. Who else would want to stalk her?

Officer Nodesky came back. ''The landlady was out in the afternoon,'' he reported. ''She had a hairdresser's appointment.''

''Which curl?'' Sam asked, breaking some of the tension, earning a smile from Nodesky. He could always manage to do that, Cait thought, when things got rough.

''She says she left a little after two o'clock and got home about four, shortly before Ms. Matthews did, and in time to hear the ruckus with your dog,'' Nodesky continued, then paused and scratched his chin. ''By the way, there's a rope attached to that tree, but no canine.''

Sam let go of Cait's hand to rub a hand over his forehead and groan. She missed his touch. She wanted to reach out for him again. She fisted her hands together in her lap, instead.

''What does that mean?'' she asked.

''That the ill-mannered monster is running hell-bent-for-leather all over Mission Creek again,'' Sam muttered.

She shot him a glance. ''Like owner, like dog. But I meant the situation with my apartment.''

''I don't run all over Mission Creek,'' Sam protested. He sounded offended.

''That's not what Dr. Leon was saying today.''

''My spot on the dance floor with her wasn't even cold before your intern jumped into it.''

Cait pulled her spine straight. ''He's hardly *my* intern.''

Officer Needles cleared her throat. "Can we get back to the situation at hand?"

Cait flushed. "Of course."

"There's really nothing we can do without any sort of ID to go on," she explained. "If your landlady had been home and we had some sort of description of anyone suspicious…" She trailed off.

Cait shrugged, feeling fragile.

"You've got good locks on your front door there," the woman said. "But I'd add one to that garage door, as well."

"I'll take care of it," Sam said.

Cait stared at him. "I'm perfectly capable of installing locks. I did the other two."

"You did the other *one*," he said. "The bottom one is crooked. That's not the work of a professional. You had someone install just the dead bolt."

He was right. She hugged herself, embarrassed. "I was saving money."

"Well, then," Officer Nodesky interrupted again. "We'll keep an eye on the place, of course, and we'll have the candle snuffer checked for prints, but there's not much else we can do at this point."

"I understand," Cait said quietly.

"Call right away if you have any other problems, or if you discover something's missing that we can trace."

"I will."

Officer Needles looked around. "With all these antiques and nothing apparently missing, it doesn't seem like a burglary," she observed.

"None of it is expensive," Cait said. "Flea-market stuff, mostly."

"Well, I didn't know that, so how would a thief?" the cop asked.

Cait nodded. The woman had a point.

When she let them out and looked back, Sam was still on the sofa. "Thank you," she said stiffly. "You can go now."

He settled back, instead, and crossed an ankle over the other knee. "Where's the remote control for your TV?"

Cait's brows lowered. "Why on earth would you want that?"

"Because I'm going to watch the news while you take a shower."

"I take my showers in the morning." She didn't trust where this was going.

He got up and prowled around the living room until he found the remote on an end table. He clicked the TV on. "Still, you'll probably want to change. You don't want to go out for dinner in scrubs."

Her heart chugged. "I'm not going out for dinner with you. I've already told you that."

"But that was before I rescued your cat from a tree."

"Your dog put him there!"

Sam sat again and flicked channels. "Still, I ought to get something out of this."

"You're conniving!"

"It's called persuasion. You've got ten minutes, Cait. If you don't leave here with me, I'm not going."

Cait backed off warily toward her bedroom and the shower. She believed him.

Or maybe she just wanted to.

Eight

They went to Coyote Harry's.

Cait's stomach heaved a little at the thought of such spicy food, but she followed Sam resolutely out of her apartment. She told herself that she just wanted to get this over with, but something in her veins fluttered, like butterflies dancing in her blood.

This was a date.

It was a date with the most eligible bachelor in the hospital, she thought, fighting off a shiver, with a man who'd already rocked her soul once and made her want to give everything she could give. She tried to tell herself again that she'd made love with him in that room because she'd thought she was going to die. But she knew, somehow she knew, that if she'd been trapped in there with Kenny Estrada, the same thing wouldn't have happened.

Sam had just changed something inside her.

The women at the hospital were buzzing about Estrada lately, but the intern couldn't hold a candle to Sam, Cait thought. Kenny's sex appeal was…forced. Sam's was as natural as the sun rising, an easy charm that came from being utterly comfortable in his skin. Sam's appreciation of women was genuine and unapologetic. He was funny, lovable and brilliant.

Now she was rhapsodizing about him. Cait stopped dead beside her car.

"What are you doing?" he asked.

Cait recovered and slid her key into the door lock. "I'm letting you feed me."

He scowled. "That's a hell of a way to put it."

"What would you like me to say?"

"How about that we're going to share an enjoyable evening together?"

Her breath hitched. "That remains to be seen."

"Well, we're not going to do it in *that*." Sam gestured at her vehicle.

Indignation tightened her spine, a reaction a whole lot better than hitching breaths and butterflies in the blood. "What's wrong with my car?"

"It's a sparrow car, and you've got more pluck than that. Come on, mine is right up the street."

Pluck? That startled her enough that she forgot the affront to her car and followed him down the driveway.

"Why aren't you parked here?" she asked when the oddity hit her.

Sam didn't answer immediately. Cait caught up with him and glanced at his face. Did he look embarrassed?

"Houdini and I were out for a drive when we decided to walk," he said after a few strides.

"You named your dog Houdini?"

"He's a magician." They started up Euclid Street side by side. "He can get out of any restraints you put him in. He was like that even as a puppy."

"Then why did you bother tying him to my tree?"

"Appearance sake."

Cait laughed.

Sam liked the sound of her laugh. Light and quick, it was almost as though it startled even her. When they'd been in that basement room, he'd tried his damnedest to coax it from her. Laughing had banished the stark fear from her eyes for a little while, and the sound of it had eased the panic and fury knotting his own midsection, as well. "Why Billy?" he asked. "That's kind of...rigid sparrowish."

Her laughter ended on a choke. "You drag me out for dinner, then you insult me?"

His gaze cut to her. "I'm being honest. 'Billy' is not creative."

She brought her chin up. "A lot you know. It's short for Billy the Kid."

He watched her chin warily. "Okay. That's creative."

They reached his car. It was red, sleek, hot, incredible. Cait's pulse shivered a little at the idea of actually riding in it, but it was a good feeling. She slid onto the rich leather of the seat with a sigh and he closed the door behind her.

"You like the concept of the Old West," he guessed when he got behind the wheel. He glanced at her and one corner of his mouth crooked up. "Desperados and cowpokes? You would have done well in Texas 130 years ago."

Cait was so startled she almost lost her breath. "I would have?"

"You've got starch."

"Is that another insult?" She was still working over the "pluck" business, not sure what to make of it. He was getting to her, she thought desperately. Cait hugged herself.

"It's a compliment. I can just picture you toting a rifle around, warning varmints off your land."

A smile got away from her. She liked the image.

"The women who followed their men to settle here were tough," Sam said. "So are you." Suddenly he thought of that business with her chin again. It wasn't arrogance or disapproval that spurred the reflex, he realized. It was courage.

She'd done it a lot in that underground room.

He pulled up the Maserati at a parking meter in front of the Tex-Mex restaurant.

"Aren't you afraid you'll come back to find the hubcaps missing?" she asked. Coyote Harry's was at the very edge of what could be considered the good part of town.

"They're insured." He shrugged.

"Does anything ever worry you?"

He thought about it. "Sure. World hunger. Holes in the ozone. Dying patients. Things worth worrying about. Not hubcaps."

Cait found herself wishing she could go through life like that. She sighed. She hoped her baby inherited some of that tendency. With the thought, she nearly tripped.

"Hey, are you okay?" Sam asked.

"I'm fine." How many times had she said that to people lately? she wondered. As though repeating it often enough would make it true.

The restaurant wasn't busy on a Monday night. They got a table right away. Something astounding happened to Cait as she sat. Her stomach rumbled with hunger this time. The smells coming from the kitchen were delicious. She'd thought this sort of food would send her rushing to the nearest washroom. Maybe it would yet. But at the moment she was ravenous, and suddenly she craved it.

She ordered fajitas and a side order of chili, forgetting that it would be chock full of the beef she usually avoided. But when Sam asked her if she wanted a beer to wash it down with, reality crashed in on her again.

"Uh, no." She asked the waitress for a glass of milk, instead.

"Beer's part of the whole experience," Sam said. "Try a Corona."

"I don't drink."

He sat back in his chair, scowling. "I think that's the first lie you've told me. Not a good foot to get started on."

"We're not starting anything." Her heart punched her breastbone. "Besides, I really don't."

"You had champagne at the ball and Ricky Mercado saw you going into a liquor store."

Cait's jaw dropped. "How do you know about that?"

"He lives next door to me."

"And you talked to him about me? I never even told him my name."

"Lucky guess."

He got that embarrassed, discomfited look on his face again. Cait watched him for a moment, wondering what it was about. Then something desperate welled up inside her. She didn't want him to think she was lying. She couldn't tell him the truth, God knew, she couldn't do that. She might have tried a beer if she wasn't pregnant. But it mattered to her that he not think she was a liar.

"I never used to drink." She flailed mentally for words. "But I stopped at the liquor store that day because…well, it was the day you cornered me in the storage room."

"'Cornered' you?"

Cait pulled her spine straight. "I was there first."

He grinned to himself, obviously pleased about something. "I got to you, then," he said.

Cait leaned back in her chair as the waitress brought her chili. "You mentioned…you talked about…" She trailed off. The smells from the bowl in front of her were heavenly. She completely forgot what she was about to say and dug in.

Sam watched her. "Cait, nobody's going to ask you to leave some for the next guy. Easy does it."

She raised her eyes to him, chewing, then swallowing. "What?"

He motioned at her bowl. "Slow down before you give yourself heartburn."

"Now you're criticizing my table manners." She put down her spoon.

"Nope. I hate women who pussyfoot around their dinner plate, nibbling on the garnish. It seriously ticks me off when they leave their meal for the kitchen dogs."

"They only had kitchen dogs in the Old West."

He grinned. "Trust me, they have them at this end of town, too."

"Well, the dogs can't have any of mine."

He threw back his head and laughed. Cait found

herself smiling, too. It delighted her when she could turn the tables on him and repay the favor a little. His humor had helped her survive three horrible days.

"I mentioned what?" he asked. "You were talking about the storage room."

She looked up as she reached for a tortilla to sop up the chili. "I beg your pardon?"

"You started to say something before you fell on that bowl like you hadn't eaten in a month. You said I talked about something."

Cait felt her blood shiver again. "Oh. You talked about...*it*."

"It?"

"What we did there in the basement."

He wiggled his brows. "It was fun, wasn't it? So why do you want to transfer to another department?"

I have to. She choked at the thought. "It was a one-time thing. And it had—has—nothing to do with our professional association."

"It doesn't have to be a one-time thing."

Cait stared at him. Her blood pounded in her ears. What was he saying? In that moment she could feel his hands on her all over again, as though weeks hadn't passed since he'd touched her. "That's what you wanted. You said so."

He drank from his beer mug as though it would drench some of the desperation he was feeling. "What if I told you that I want to start all over again? That I want to go back to before we met in the lobby on your first day back to work and have a fresh start?"

Cait grabbed her milk and gulped. "We can't do that."

"Why not?"

"It's an escapable fact that you can't turn back time."

"The human mind can do anything it wants to do. You're proof positive of that."

"Me?" she asked. Just then the waitress brought her fajitas. Cait looked up at her with a world of gratitude for the interruption.

"You," Sam said after the waitress deposited their plates. He wouldn't let the subject drop.

"I'm practical," she squeaked. "I move ahead."

"And that's admirable. Let's face it, otherwise you could have turned into another Branson Hines. But going back isn't always bad, either."

Hines? "I would never hurt anyone like he did!" She was horrified.

"That's my point. He's nasty and bitter about the cards life dealt him."

She tried to wait while he cut into his chimichanga. But she was too hungry. She took another bite of her food.

"You had rough beginnings," Sam said.

She closed her eyes briefly. "I talked too much in that underground room."

He ignored that. "Look at someone like me, for example. I can't take the kind of credit you can for where I've landed in life."

"But you're a doctor."

"All the opportunities for that were given to me. You made yours."

Suddenly, absurdly, she wanted to cry. "I did that, yes." She closed her eyes briefly. She wasn't sure anyone had ever complimented her so much.

"Cait, you're an incredible woman. I just want a chance with you."

She looked at him. His eyes looked as if he meant it. But she couldn't let herself believe it. "Why are you saying these things? You can't need a nurse that badly."

Sam felt something warm and helpless move over him. "No. I don't. I just don't want you to close the door on us."

The waitress chose that moment to come back to their table. "Dessert?" she asked brightly.

Sam looked at Cait's denuded plate. Whoever thought she could eat like that, the little sparrow? "Two of everything," he said to the woman.

Cait sat back quickly. "Oh, no. I'm full now."

"The sopapillas are terrific," he said. "With coffee."

She shook her head firmly. "Too much cholesterol. And caffeine."

"Cait."

Her gaze shot to him. "What?"

"It's an undeniable fact that if we spend our entire lifetimes only putting the proper things in our bodies, a truck will come along and flatten us. *Something* is going to get you."

"Not if I can help it."

He laughed and realized that this was the best night he'd had in a very long time.

"So what do you say about that transfer?" he asked when he finally paid the bill.

"I'm moving over to Dr. Eckle's unit on Wednesday."

"You really think so?"

Her eyes chastised him. They were so calm, so blue, so sure, he thought. "Yes. But thanks for the meal."

He felt frustration tug at him. "Damn it, Cait, it makes no sense for you to transfer."

Something between sadness and determination moved in her eyes. "Yes, it does."

"Then explain it to me."

She hesitated. "I can't."

One look at her jaw told him he wasn't going to get any more out of her. Damn it, what was going on here? Then his ex-wife's words came back to him. *That patented Sam sex appeal.*

He didn't know what else to try.

"Okay," he said equably. "Are you ready? Let's go."

She blinked at him. "Okay?"

"You want the transfer. I give up. I'll take you home."

He watched as she stood and gathered up her purse. She looked back at the table a little longingly. "You didn't leave anything for a doggy bag," he pointed out.

"I was thinking about taking some scraps for Houdini."

"He's in Oklahoma by now."

She looked at him, wide-eyed. "Are you serious?"

"Yes and no. But he'll be back on my doorstep before midnight with a bill from the dogcatcher in his mouth."

"Why do you even own a dog?" she asked.

He found himself seriously thinking about it as he unlocked the passenger door of his car for her. His hubcaps were all still in place, which he considered a minor miracle. Maybe she was some kind of good-luck angel. They'd come out of that basement room alive, after all.

"I grew up with four brothers and sisters," he explained finally.

Cait felt her heart spasm as she got into the car. "That sounds so nice."

Nice? He thought of the fistfights over first dibs for the bathroom. The absolute brawls over only two legs per turkey. He didn't answer until he pulled away from the curb. "You'll meet them someday." Where the hell had that come from? he thought. He continued quickly. "I don't like a quiet house. Houdini keeps my condo lively."

"Did you have him when you were married?"

His gaze cut to her as he drove. "That's right, I forgot. You met Nancy."

She nodded. "What went wrong with your marriage?" She was immediately mortified by the question. It was none of her business. She couldn't let herself care.

"Houdini," he said complacently.

"Then I can't blame her for leaving you. He's awful."

Sam laughed, then he took a hand from the wheel to scrub the smile from his mouth. He decided to answer honestly. "I left her," he said finally. "I got bored. After that happened, I was afraid that if I stayed married, I'd end up like my parents."

She frowned. "What's wrong with your parents?"

"They're bored," he repeated.

Cait frowned as though she couldn't understand the concept.

"With themselves. With life," he explained. He pulled into her driveway and stopped the car, then he put the transmission in neutral and pulled up the emergency break. "I never want to be like that."

"Sam, you take life by storm."

"Or it tackles me, I'm not sure which."

Suddenly Cait saw the truth in his eyes. She saw shadows move there. "Sam, you can't seriously blame yourself for what happened to us with Hines."

For a heartbeat she didn't think he would answer. Then he looked away out his window. "Let's put it this way. Jared Cross managed to get Melanie and the others away from Hines. Jake White got us free."

"Tabitha did that. Although poor Billy will never be the same for it."

"Jake saved us and Tabitha Monroe."

"Why would you think that?" She pressed her hands to her cheeks. "You are such a *man*."

"Yeah, I am. And you do something to me, Cait. I'm not sure what it is or even if I like it, but you do. And it eats at me that I let you down."

Things inside her started to stiffen. Other parts of her started to soften. "What are you saying?"

"That it has to be resolved before it drives me out of my mind."

"It's over now. Behind us." But she thought again of someone having been in her apartment today. Was it over?

"I wasn't talking about him. I was talking about us."

She saw him leaning closer to her, almost in slow

motion. Like the first time he had kissed her. She'd stared at him then, too, mesmerized, not really believing he would do it. She didn't believe he was going to do it now, either.

But he did. His mouth found hers.

And it was all the same. The fierce, ready heat that gathered inside her, almost hurting. The sensation that she had been waiting for this moment all her life. The gentle skim of his mouth over hers, the warmth of the contact, made something happen to her. Her head fell back a little and she opened to him.

Then his hands were in her hair, on both sides of her head, holding her still for the sweetest assault she could imagine. His mouth closed over hers, harder and more intent. His tongue dipped past her teeth, and something wild and hungry reared inside her, something that had her fisting the front of his shirt in both her hands. She came a little out of her seat to lean into him.

All of her, the very essence of her, crashed over him again. Sam forgot that this was supposed to be part of his plan to lure her back to him. He was lost in her scent. The silk of her hair slid between his fingers. Her breasts nudged warmly and gently against his chest.

There was no room inside him for fear that no other woman had ever been able to do this to him. Not now. His need for her was too great to allow it. He lifted her the rest of the way out of her seat, pulling her into his arms, on top of him. She wriggled for a more comfortable position as her tongue started meeting his and she deepened the kiss of her own will. Her clever little fingers danced over his chest, his shoulders, into his hair.

"Inside," he groaned against her mouth. "Let's go inside."

Cait froze.

She went utterly still before she reared off him, landing hard in her own seat again. She gasped. "What did I just do?"

"Whatever it was, I liked it." He tried to grin, but he was shaken, too.

He wasn't ready for the way she shoved blindly against her door or the way she flew out of the car. The crack of the door slamming shut made him flinch as though someone had struck him. His blood was still roaring. He watched her run to her stairs and take the first four of them pretty much the way she had come down them earlier—at a leap.

He never had a chance to stop her.

Sam thought briefly of going after her. But by the time he got to the top of her stairs, he knew she'd have the door locked and bolted as tightly as a sixteenth-century chastity belt.

Besides, his legs didn't feel steady enough to carry him.

What the hell was going on here? Why did he want her so desperately, and why was she equally determined to set him aside? What was he going to do about it?

Giving up, walking away, never occurred to him. Sam eased the Maserati back out of her driveway, scrambling for still another alternative plan. He hoped the next one left him breathing better than this one had.

* * *

Cait was sick in the morning.

She told herself it was the pregnancy. All those hormones. She stepped out of the shower and dove for the toilet, letting nature take its course. She eased back to sit against the wall for a moment, then she got up shakily to brush her teeth.

She'd barely slept a wink. She was exhausted and she looked it. She caught her reflection in the mirror and winced. There were vague purple smudges under her eyes.

He'd kissed her again. And she had melted into him, had swarmed all over him, just as she had the first time. Her legs wobbled. Cait sat down hard on the rim of the tub.

The truth pounded at her. She hadn't been pregnant the first time she'd flung herself at him. And she hadn't had PTSD then. She'd just…craved him.

And she had craved him again last night.

It was him, she thought desperately. It wasn't anything else, any of these other things that were going on in her life right now. It was something in the way she reacted to him. A lifetime full of caution was hurled aside when he was near. Twenty-five years of common sense deserted her. He got close to her and she wanted. She ached. She needed. Even knowing how foolish and how dangerous wanting and aching and needing could be.

She only had to get through one more day with Sam before her transfer went into effect, she told herself, trying for calm. She would just give him as wide a berth today as possible. But something painful bloomed in her chest at the thought of never working with him again, of escaping to Laredo and never seeing him again.

By the time she got to the hospital, she was steadier. Her stomach had settled. She checked on Beatty Jansen and spent a few minutes chatting with the girl. She was early again, so she went downstairs for a cup of tea before her shift started. She was sipping diligently when Nancy Walters approached her table.

Cait tried hard not to groan, but the sound came out, anyway. Nancy plunked a cup of coffee on the table and sat across from her, rubbing her feet just as she had before.

"They can't possibly hurt you already," Cait snapped. "It's not even eight o'clock yet." *Did he ever kiss you like that?* The question vaulted into her mind from out of nowhere. *And if he did, how did you ever let him go?*

"Habit." Nancy grinned a little sheepishly and pushed her feet back into her shoes. "You know, I'm not your enemy, Cait. If anyone is, it's Sam."

Cait felt her heart chug. "What do you mean?"

"Bert Eckle declined your transfer about five minutes ago. Actually, I came to the cafeteria looking for you so I could tell you in person. I know it meant a lot to you."

It took Cait a moment to process what the woman was saying. "My transfer's not going through? Why?"

Nancy sipped her coffee. "I just told you. Dr. Eckle rethought the idea of letting Elizabeth Halverson go."

"Why?"

"Do you want his excuse, or do you want to know what I think?"

Cait ground her teeth together. "Both."

"Okay. He says Beth's got a real rapport going with a touch-and-go preemie."

Cait narrowed her eyes. "But you don't believe him."

"No. Because I know Sam."

"You think he's behind this?"

"All I'm saying is that the man has never wanted one single thing he didn't get. And he observes no laws."

"There's a first time for everything." Cait forgot about her tea and pushed to her feet.

"What are you going to do?" Nancy asked.

"Hurt him."

"Can I watch?"

Cait shot her a killer look. "No." She stalked out of the cafeteria.

Nancy sat back in her chair speculatively. "Well," she said. "Good for you."

Nine

The last thing Cait felt like doing on her lunch break was keeping her appointment with Jared Cross. She trudged down the hallway at a little past noon, her nerves screwing tighter with every step.

He would take one look at her and know, she thought inanely.

There would be something in her stance, her posture, her eyes, that would scream loud and clear, "I'm having Sam's baby!" Or maybe, Cait thought, Cross would spy the wanton, sex-crazed woman who peered out from inside her eyes, the one who couldn't seem to keep her hands off Sam Walters no matter how hard she tried. It had occurred to her over the course of the morning that she had to end her professional relationship with Dr. Cross now as well. It was bad enough that she wouldn't be able to escape Sam, after all, until she left Mission Creek. The thought of dodging Cross's intrusive questions at the same time left her mentally exhausted.

She braced herself and knocked on Cross's door. His voice called to her to come in and she stepped inside.

"How are you doing today?" he asked.

"Just dandy."

He studied her as though making sure that was

true. "Good. To be frank, you worried me running out of the ball like that the other night."

"Oh, that. My apartment survived. Everything is fine." Cait sat neatly and smoothed the legs of her pale-yellow scrubs.

"You mean with the candle?"

"The candle," she agreed, "and everything else, too, for that matter. Everything's perfect now."

He still looked skeptical. "No more bursts of anger?"

She thought of the way she had taken Sam's head off four hours ago because he had blocked her transfer. He'd denied it of course, which had only made her more frustrated and furious. "No," she said, but her voice was a little too high-pitched. Apparently lies weren't coming *that* easily to her these days. Maybe she really was getting back to herself.

Cait cleared her throat carefully. "Well, yes," she confessed. "But this time it was warranted."

"Care to tell me about it so I can decide?"

"Uh, no."

"Caitlyn, I'm your doctor." He gave that sigh again. It occurred to Cait that he did that a lot with her. "You can trust me. In fact, if you don't trust me, then we're wasting our time here."

"Actually, I've been thinking about that." She plucked an invisible piece of lint off her knee. "I'm not sure it's necessary for me to continue with this."

"You want to curtail our sessions?"

"I just don't have time for these PTSD symptoms any longer."

"And you think that such a decision will just make them go away?"

"Do you know you answer almost all of my comments with questions?" she countered.

Cross grinned. "That's what shrinks do. So, answer me."

"About the symptoms?" She sat back in her chair and crossed her arms over her breasts in an unconsciously defensive posture. "I can make them go away if I don't humor them."

He shook his head. "No, Caitlyn, you can't."

Her chin jutted forward. "Yes, I can."

He laughed. "If it were that easy, I'd be out of a job."

She smiled slightly. "Most people aren't as strong-willed as I am. I think you're safe."

He leaned forward and put his elbows on his desk. "You *have* changed, you know."

Cait thought about denying it and knew it would be senseless. So she took another tack. "I'm not sure that's a bad thing."

"I'm not, either."

She blinked at him, surprised. "So I'm done here?"

"If you insist. I can't hold you to therapy."

She thought about it. "No, you can't."

"It just concerns me that you're ending our professional association because there's something you don't want me to know."

Cait shivered a little and wondered if he noticed. She decided not to try to answer that one. "I've done everything you told me to do," she said, instead. "I went to the storage room and to the ball, and I'm coming along."

"Caitlyn, you didn't speak to one single person at

that ball who was involved in the Hines situation with you.''

"But I never really talked to them before then, either,'' she pointed out reasonably. She was pleased when he looked startled by that. "And it's not true, anyway. I spoke to Sam. Dr. Walters,'' she amended quickly.

"I think skirmishing would be a more accurate reflection of what you two were doing that night,'' Cross said. "You do know that that sort of squabbling often indicates suppressed sexual tension, right?''

Cait choked. She'd been right! He'd taken one look at her and had glimpsed the sex maniac in her unplumbed depths! She wondered what he would say if he knew she'd had dinner with Sam last night and had flung herself all over him. She didn't dare even think about it. If she thought about it, it might show on her face.

"Not in this case,'' she said carefully.

Cross got to his feet, defeated. "Okay, have it your way. But I'm here if you need me.''

Cait stood, as well. "Thank you.'' She thought briefly of telling him that she would be moving shortly, anyway, just to make him feel better about her cutting off her treatment. But she still wasn't absolutely sure he wouldn't repeat something like that to Tabitha or, worse, to Sam. He might just consider it common knowledge. She pressed her lips shut and went with him to the door.

"Promise me one thing,'' he said, opening it. "If your symptoms change in any way, get in touch with me immediately.''

Cait stepped into the hall, frowning. "How would they change?"

"So far everything you've been experiencing has been on a manageable level. But if the PTSD exacerbates, it could be an indication that you really need to deal with it more aggressively."

Cait stood straighter. "That won't happen to me."

Another flickering grin touched his mouth. "Yes. It could even happen to you."

She didn't want to ask and did, anyway. "You're saying everything could get worse?"

"It could. It's only been a few weeks since you escaped from that room. So far, for instance, you haven't experienced any dreams reliving the ordeal." He looked at her sharply to make sure that was correct.

Cait shook her head. "No, I haven't."

"Or outright panic attacks?"

"Nothing like that." She'd come unglued yesterday when she'd realized someone had actually gone into her apartment, but she'd had damned good cause. And she didn't want to tell him about that, either. He might think the whole thing had been a product of her imagination and that she was indeed getting worse. Then he'd insist that she keep seeing him.

"Okay, then," Cross said. "Those are some parameters. If you start dreaming of Hines or find yourself incapable of walking down the street without hyperventilating, let me know."

"I will," she promised.

He went back into his office and closed the door again. Cait hurried off down the hall.

Now that that was over, it occurred to her that she actually did feel pretty good. She felt stronger than she had since Hines had grabbed her. She had plans now, many plans. Sam had derailed her somewhat with his high-handed shenanigans with Dr. Eckle. But in the end, she'd win that issue because he couldn't stop her from quitting her job. And leaving town would have an added advantage: she'd escape whoever had taken it into his head to break into her apartment.

She reached the nurses' station, unaware that she was rubbing the back of her neck again. She glanced over her shoulder, back up the hallway, without realizing it.

"How's Beatty?" she asked Angelina Moffit.

Sam's voice answered from behind her. "I can release her tomorrow."

Cait turned about a little too quickly and felt dizzy. "Oh, that's good." She had to put a hand on the desk to steady herself. Then she fell into those eyes of his. Their earlier spat over him blocking her transfer was apparently forgotten. His eyes were warm, a little searching....

Then they sharpened as he noticed the way she was bracing herself. "Are you okay?"

Cait snatched her hand back. "Fine."

"No more incidents like last night?"

Cait felt her heart slam. "I don't go around behaving like that as a matter of course."

He looked startled, then he grinned. "Glad to hear it. I do believe, Nurse Matthews, that you just paid me a compliment. But I was talking about your apartment, not what happened after dinner."

"Oh." Cait was mortified. "Of course you were."

"But *you* weren't." He wiggled his brows.

"Yes, I was."

"Liar."

She couldn't keep a straight face. What was he doing to her? "Don't make me laugh," she said desperately.

"Why not? It's good for the soul."

"I'm still mad at you."

He leaned negligently against the nurses' station. "I keep telling you I didn't do anything."

She gave a huffing breath. "Liar."

He laughed. "So what are you doing tonight, Nurse Matthews?"

"Tonight?" she echoed, her breath catching.

"Let's have dinner again."

"You want to eat out two nights in a row?"

"Why not?"

"Well, because…it's wasteful."

He leaned closer to her until their noses almost touched and she could see the green flecks in his eyes. Something inside her shook. "Cait," he said, "I'm a bachelor. I eat in one of two ways. I go out, or I order in. So join me."

"You should learn to cook," she said inanely, struggling frantically for her breath.

"Then come over tonight and teach me."

"No."

He wasn't moving back, wasn't giving her any space. "Why not?" he asked.

"Last night was a one-time thing."

"We thought that everything that went on in the

basement room was, too, but I changed your mind about that.''

She couldn't get air. Cait looked around frantically. "Sam, not here."

He looked pleased with himself. "My place it is, then. Seven o'clock. We'll continue the discussion this evening." He sauntered off down the corridor.

"I said no!" she shouted after him. "I only agreed last night because of Billy. And damn it, I'm still mad at you!"

She heard his laughter, but he didn't turn around to respond. Gradually Cait became aware of that feeling again, the sensation that someone was watching her.

She looked around. At least six members of the staff were staring at her.

"He just rescued my cat," she explained helplessly. Then she hurried off to see to the afternoon meds.

The woman had thought long and hard about the best way to proceed after discovering the pregnancy test. There were so many variables. But as she watched Cait practically run down the hall to the drug room after talking to Sam, she considered her dilemma solved.

She smiled, but the reflex vanished quickly, going brittle and ugly and hard.

Some people had all the luck. They got abducted and they still landed on their feet, whole and unharmed, pregnant and with a killer-handsome physician fawning at their feet. What did that anal-retentive little twit have that *she* didn't?

Sam, she answered herself. And a baby.

She'd watched them attack each other in his car last night outside Cait's apartment. She'd gone back to make sure that her little detour through the place had gone unnoticed—which, to her alarm, it hadn't—and she'd seen them leave together. She'd waited and they'd come back together, too. They'd stayed in his car. Groping. Touching. Kissing.

Something hot pounded at the woman's temples. At first, she had hated all of them, everyone who had put her in this position—useless, barren, alone, with huge needs that went unanswered. But since she'd found that pregnancy test yesterday, her fury had focused.

Cait Matthews was her problem.

She herself could have had Sam, given enough time. She could have gotten out of this miserable predicament of her life. But none of that was likely to happen now because the prim little perfect nurse had his child.

The woman wondered if Sam knew yet. From the tone of the last conversation they'd just had, she didn't think so.

She considered that she might let him in on the secret somehow. But that didn't actually advance her position. He was already in love with the twit; he just didn't know it yet. Once he knew about the baby, he would be all over little Cait. The woman was sure of that. Better, she thought, to derail Nurse Matthews before Sam ever found out.

She wondered how to do that, and then it came to her. What if *she* had that baby, not Cait Matthews?

The idea spread through her head like floodlights

being snapped on in every corner. She left the threshold of the supply room where she'd been watching from, walking as though in a trance, playing the scenario out in her mind. She already knew she couldn't get pregnant, though heaven knew, she'd tried. But judging from that pregnancy test, there was a baby available if she played her cards right. A baby would give her back everything. She might even decide that she didn't need Sam Walters, after all, if she had a baby of her own. What could he give her if she already had everything?

A baby would restore her old life.

If Cait Matthews lost her mind, she wouldn't be able to keep the infant. If Sam didn't know it was his, he wouldn't take it, either. But a friend might be entrusted to care for it. And then she could just...disappear with it.

Or maybe the state would force Caitlyn to hand the baby over if she was proved mentally incompetent. How difficult could it be to steal a child out of foster care? All those people cared about were the stipends the government paid them for each kid.

The woman began walking faster, toward the nurses' locker area that was at the far end of the central corridor. It was time, she decided, to push Cait Matthews over the edge.

She had checked this out, too, when she'd peeked at Cait's file. Her locker was number twelve. The woman found it, then groped in her pockets for something to write on. She found her grocery list and flipped it over. There was a chalkboard in the room, where the nurses left memos to each other. The woman grabbed the pink chalk there and snapped it in two. With the thin end, she began writing:

I KNOW ABOUT YOUR BABY. WATCH OUT. THEY TAKE BABIES AWAY FROM CRAZY WOMEN.

She grinned, folded the note in half and pushed it through one of the vents in Cait's locker. She was very, very glad that she had noticed the nurse coming out of Dr. Cross's office a little while ago and had eavesdropped on their discussion.

All things came to those who waited, the woman thought. She let out a sigh, put the chalk back and dusted her hands on her thighs.

She was *not* going to have dinner with him again, Cait thought, heading for her locker at the end of the day. Every solid, determined thing inside her wanted to fold and melt at the thought of being alone with him again, of touching him again. She couldn't risk it. She didn't dare.

On the other hand, what could she possibly do to avoid it? She had the excuse that she didn't know where he lived so she couldn't go over there, but she also knew that he would have no qualms about coming to get her. Cait pushed into the locker room. She realized she was wringing her hands and she fisted them. Determination, she thought. Backbone. Pluck and starch and unplumbed depths. She would just take *herself* out for dinner, she decided, then she wouldn't be home when he came banging at her door.

She chewed at her lip, her heart sinking slowly with the decision. Was there any harm, really, in seeing him just another time or two before she moved away, of savoring what she could before spending the rest of her life alone?

What was she thinking? Besides, she wouldn't be alone. Never again. She'd have her baby.

Cait yanked open her locker. A little piece of paper was stuck in the vent, but it was jarred loose by the movement and it fluttered to the floor. She stared at it and didn't know whether to laugh or to cry. She pressed a shaking hand to her mouth. Damn you, Sam. He'd crept in here and had left his address for her so she'd have no excuse.

She was overwhelmed that he would be that determined over her. She told herself that his fascination with her would wear off eventually. Even he had pretty much said last night that that was his tendency. If she let herself be taken in by it, it would break her heart. But still, this was sweet. Touching.

She bent down and plucked the piece of paper off the floor, pressing it against her chest for a moment. Then she finally sighed and opened it.

I KNOW ABOUT YOUR BABY. WATCH OUT. THEY TAKE BABIES AWAY FROM CRAZY WOMEN.

Cait gave a little cry and dropped the note as though it had bitten her. She reared away from it until her spine crashed into the locker behind her. The metal rang.

"No, no, no," she whispered. She closed her eyes and opened them again. The note was still there.

But no one knew about the baby.

She went to her knees and snatched it up again.

Maybe she really was crazy. Maybe she was flaming mad. Maybe all that was written there was Sam's address and she was seeing things now, hallucinating. She would run right back to Dr. Cross. She would risk him guessing everything. "Just please," she groaned, "let the note say something else."

The same words stared back at her.

She started ripping it. First in big pieces, then in smaller and smaller ones. She gathered them up in her trembling hands and carried them into the lavatory. She dropped them into one of the toilets and flushed.

A few tiny pieces remained. She flushed again until every trace of the note was gone.

Someone knew. How? No one could possibly know! She hadn't even been to the doctor yet!

She really was losing her mind. Then she realized that this meant just the opposite, and her limbs went to stone. This was *proof.*

Someone really was watching her, following her, creeping through her apartment. They knew her most intimate secret. They knew she was pregnant. And they knew she'd been seeing Jared Cross. Cait scrubbed her hand frantically over the back of her neck and returned to the locker room. She peered down every aisle until she was sure she was alone.

No one was going to take this baby from her. If her behavior was a little erratic...well, pregnant women got that way and no one ran around snatching their babies from them. That was absurd.

She breathed hard, fast, deep, thinking it through.

The note was gone. She would put it out of her mind and go on with her plans. Because, in the end, there was nothing she could do about it, nothing at all. She couldn't go to the police with it and she couldn't tell Sam. Because they'd all want to know what the note had said.

And if someone was watching her, then they could damned well go to hell before she'd let them know they'd terrified her. She wouldn't act even the slightest bit ruffled, the slightest bit crazy.

Cait gathered her purse out of her locker. She locked it again meticulously. Then she went back to the lavatory to peer at her reflection in the mirror. She slapped some color into her cheeks and left the room.

She was halfway across the lobby when she heard a voice call her name. Cait paused and looked back. It was Tabitha. Her friend hurried to catch up with her.

"Hey, are you all right?"

Cait pasted a wide smile on her face. "Of course. Why?"

"I called you three times and you just kept walking."

"I have a hundred things on my mind."

Tabitha grabbed both her shoulders. "I've been worried sick about you. Jake said that someone broke into your apartment yesterday."

Cait's stomach squeezed. She so badly wanted to trust her. Tabitha was the closest thing to a friend she'd ever had. But she steeled herself. "I think I was mistaken."

"How can you be mistaken about something like that?"

Cait waved a hand. "I just got paranoid because

Billy was outside. But you know what? This morning, as I was leaving, he did it again.''

"Did what?''

"Darted right out the door. As soon as I get home, I'll call the police and tell them I overreacted and apologize for wasting their time.''

Tabitha looked skeptical. "Billy doesn't dart. He's too fat to dart.''

"I've had him on a diet.''

Tabitha laughed. "Oh, he must love that. Those few days I had him while you were in trouble, he ate every leftover scrap in the kitchen he could find.''

Cait nodded, feeling a little desperate from holding up the charade. But she didn't know who was watching her, who was listening. She couldn't let anyone know she was taking any of this seriously. She couldn't act frightened and deranged.

"Well,'' she said, "I've got to go.''

Tabitha squinted at her. "Are you sure there's nothing you want to talk about?''

Cait blinked innocently. "Why would there be?''

"I'm just curious. I heard you put in for a transfer from Sam.''

"Nancy Walters has a very big mouth.''

"Actually, Sam told me.''

"He can't be trusted, either.''

Tabitha grinned. "And you two were seen tooling around town in his Maserati last night.''

Cait grabbed her friend's arm hard. "By who? Who saw me?'' Who's watching me?

"Hey, easy does it.'' Tabitha disengaged her grip. "It was Jake.''

"Oh.'' Cait let out the breath she was holding.

"You know, there's an awful lot going on in your life lately that I don't know about. Let's have dinner and talk."

"I—" Cait broke off suddenly as she started to beg off. It was exactly what she had been planning to do. She needed to stay away from home for a while to elude Sam. "That's a wonderful idea."

Tabitha looked startled, then she smiled. "Good. Let me just run back to my office and get my things."

"I'll wait here."

Tabitha hurried off. Cait concentrated on nonchalantly studying the decor. No one could know, she kept telling herself.

The woman was beside herself. Damn it, Cait Matthews should be a sobbing, uncontrollable ball of nerves right now! Hadn't she seen the note? Instead, she chatted, she smiled, she wandered around the lobby waiting, looking as though she hadn't a care in the world.

"You're crazy, damn it," she whispered. "You're crazy as a loon. And your baby is mine."

Well, then, she thought, apparently the perfect little nurse needed another nudge out of sanity. The woman left the lobby to set about putting a whole new plan in motion.

Ten

The very first thing Cait did when she got home from dinner was cancel her appointment with the Laredo obstetrician. She called and left a message with his answering service. Then she dutifully put herself to bed for a good night's sleep and stared at the ceiling.

Near dawn, she finally gave up on sleep, which had been fitful at best. She went into the bathroom and leaned over the basin to splash cold water on her face. Then she trudged into the kitchen for the decaffeinated tea she'd bought. A few sips left her feeling marginally better.

Somehow, through the night, she'd managed to put a few pieces together—or at least she thought she had. How many times in the hospital had she had the urge to look over her shoulder? It had happened here, as well, in her own home. Obviously someone really had been hovering nearby all those times. They'd been listening when she'd placed her call to the obstetrician—from work, at a pay phone in the pediatrics lounge on her lunch break. Someone had overheard her making the appointment.

That purely terrified her. She had to find a different doctor now. She couldn't take any chances.

She didn't know what kind of harm this person meant for her or her baby.

She decided to put in for a sick day and drive to Laredo on Friday. She could make a new appointment with someone else in person. And she'd spend the rest of that day looking for an apartment and a new job.

She heard a mewling sound and realized that it came from her own throat. She was going to miss Sam so much.

Her spine snapped straight with that thought. Sam? Not Tabitha? Well, Tabitha, too, she thought. Their dinner last night had been just what she'd needed to get her mind off everything. But she hadn't confided in Tabitha about this nightmare because Tabitha wasn't the one who had seen her fall apart the day someone had broken into her home. Tabitha hadn't spent that hideous time with her in Hines's underground room. That had been Sam, there whenever she'd needed him. He had touched her and made love to her, had made her laugh. Somehow, through it all, he had crawled past every one of her defenses and left her aching for more.

Last night she'd gotten home to find brownies on her doorstep. The note he'd left had said he'd tried to cook on his own.

Cait laughed a little hoarsely, then closed her eyes. She wished, oh, how she wished, that she could teach him to cook. And that she could believe he would stay around afterward.

She went back to her bedroom and peeled off her nightgown to take a shower. She had to be strong.

* * *

Cait managed to keep that thought in her head until Sam cornered her in the meds room just before her shift ended. As she stood on tiptoe looking for something on a high shelf, she heard the door shut behind her. She gasped, thinking the worst, her heart hurtling. She looked around.

"Oh." She let her breath out shakily. "It's only you."

"Thanks for that." Sam looked vaguely affronted. "Who were you expecting?"

Cait shrugged carefully and changed the subject. "What's that in your hand?"

He held up her day-off request. "What's this about?"

Cait hugged herself. Why couldn't she achieve even one little thing without a confrontation with him? She was starting to feel desperate. "I still have nine sick days stockpiled," she said. "I thought I would use one."

"You know you're going to be sick on Friday?"

She felt her temper twitch. "Okay, then call it a personal day."

"What do you have to do that can't be done on a weekend?"

"You know, you can be very domineering. And nosy. It's none of your business."

"That's what you said about switching to another doctor, but it wasn't true."

"Well, it's true this time."

He raked his fingers through his hair, looking abashed and irritated all at once. "I'm just curious."

"Okay. I'm running off to marry a sheik."

He didn't laugh. His jaw only tightened. "Where did you go last night?"

She shrugged. "Same sheik."

"Damn it, Cait!"

She threw her hands in the air. "What do you want me to say?"

"I want you to confide in me!"

"Why?"

"I don't know!" he shouted back.

Suddenly Cait heard Jared Cross's voice again. *You do know that that sort of squabbling often indicates suppressed sexual attraction.* She felt her skin heat. Then something else struck her and almost knocked her knees out from under her.

He wanted to know everything she was doing and why, and he was irritated that she wouldn't tell him. He was acting like a jealous, frustrated lover.

"Errands," she said quickly to get that possibility right out of her mind. "I have some errands that have accumulated, the kind of things that can only be done on weekdays."

"Oh."

"And last night I had dinner with Tabitha."

"Monroe?"

"Yes. How many Tabithas do we know? Are you going to check out my story?"

"Why would I do that?"

"I don't know, Sam. Why are you asking me in the first place?"

Their eyes met and her heart shifted. What she saw in his gaze was a man in misery, a man who didn't understand what he was feeling and who no longer recognized himself in his own skin. How could that be? Her knees felt weak. Cait dragged over a foot-stool and sat on it.

"By the way," she said thinly to change the subject, "those brownies were terrible."

"I know." He leaned back against the door, looking glum. "Houdini was batting them around the kitchen floor like they were hockey pucks."

"He batted the ones you gave me?"

"Why? Did you actually eat one?"

She shook her head. "I couldn't. Not without chipping a tooth."

"It's your fault, you know. We were supposed to have dinner. You stood me up."

"I said no."

"Why?" he demanded. "Why are you fighting this?"

"Because I don't know why you're pushing it!" The words were bald, blurted and took even her by surprise. Cait flushed.

"To tell you the truth, neither do I."

She laughed shakily. "Then we have something in common."

"The question is, what do we do about it?"

She stood. "For my part, I'm going home to feed my cat. He found your brownies to be somewhat lacking in the goody department."

"Cait…"

She got to the door and wrenched it open. Then she looked back at him. Her heart was keening. "Please, Sam. Please, just let it be." Then she strode off.

By nine o'clock, Cait was exhausted. She took a book to bed, determined to keep her eyes open until ten. There was something abnormal about a grown, single woman going to sleep before at least one evening-news program, she thought drearily. Then she wondered when she had started doubting the orderly, sweet routine of her life.

When suddenly it was no longer enough, she realized.

The answer jarred her and she got up for a glass of milk. She passed the picture of her mother on the dresser and paused to pick it up. Steadiness had always been her greatest treasure, she thought, blinking back sudden tears. But her whole world was upside down now.

All she'd ever wanted was peace. Monotony had come to her with a price. She'd fought hard for it. She didn't want to move to Laredo, because she'd already jumped from home to home so many times in her life she'd needed her own zip code. She didn't want to love, because she didn't want anyone else to ever leave her again and go away.

But she was moving because she had to—to protect herself and her child. And she was pretty sure she was falling in love with Sam whether she liked it or not.

Shaken, Cait went back to bed without getting the milk. She turned her bedside light out and was asleep before shadows gathered in the corners of her room again. Then, somewhere in the darkness, she heard his voice again. Hines's.

"Don't give me a hard time. I'll hurt you. I'll snap you in two."

Cait groaned and rolled over in her sleep.

"You're mine. You'll always be mine. You'll do what I say, when I say it."

"No," she murmured, struggling up from sleep.

The darkness of her bedroom pressed in on her. Safe, she realized, her heart thudding; she was safe. She was home in her own apartment. But perspiration clung to her skin like dew. Then she heard him again.

"Plan all you want. You'll never get away from me."

Cait emitted a cry and threw the covers off her. She scrambled over the edge and to her feet. He was here! She fumbled for her bedside light and turned it on. Electricity speared through the room, illuminating it.

No one was there. The clock read 1:52.

"You're mine," Hines said.

His voice was coming from the other room. Suddenly Cait was a madwoman. She looked around frantically for something she could use as a weapon. There was nothing. She dashed into her closet and came up with the high-heeled shoe she'd worn to the dance. Hines wasn't a spider to be squashed. She knew that. He was a treacherous, cruel human being. But the shoe was all she had. If she could startle him enough with it, maybe she could get to a knife in the kitchen.

She gave a howl of pure fury and ran that way. The sound ricocheted off her ceiling and seemed to echo off her walls.

"I'll come back to you soon enough," he said.

The kitchen. Cait lunged that way. She was ready to find him, to fight him, to tear him apart. She stumbled into the kitchen and threw on the lights.

And still, there was no one.

She stood, trembling, listening, clutching her shoe. It had all been in her mind. But it had seemed so real.

Dr. Cross had said that the PTSD might get worse, that she could dream.

Cait made a keening sound of despair. She really was losing her mind. She thought she could actually feel something breaking inside her with the realization. All her resolve. All her determination. The break-in, the feelings that someone was watching her...all of that, she knew, was really as insubstantial as Hines's ghost was now in her kitchen. The note wasn't proof, after all, *because she didn't have it anymore.*

Cait grabbed the kitchen phone. She leaned back against the wall and felt her legs folding. She sat, melting into a puddle on the floor, ashamed and scared. For a long time she only held the phone against her chest.

Then she called Sam.

Sam wasn't sleeping, though he knew he'd regret it in the morning. He was in his kitchen with his heels up on the table, leaning back in one of the chairs, a photo album in his lap. It depicted life, he thought, as he had known it.

There were pictures of his parents, and some of them dated back forty-five years. He looked hard for a smile on either of their faces and actually found a few this time. He went through photos from the various weddings of his three sisters—two apiece—and snapshots of his brother in China. Max was in the

Peace Corps and probably a lot happier for it, foot-loose and fancy-free.

It was a ritual Sam undertook whenever he felt himself getting shaky. Whenever he was seeing a woman who seemed to have him by the throat. Normally he looked at these pictures and, as Nancy had said, broke out in hives. This time it didn't work. He found himself staring at the pictures for something he might have missed before. Something that would explain why, with every moment he spent with her, he wanted Cait more and more.

Then the phone rang, scattering his thoughts. Startled, Sam glanced at his watch. It was two o'clock in the morning. No phone call was ever good in the wee hours. It meant a patient had taken a turn for the worse or—

Then he knew. It was Cait. His blood froze.

He came up out of the chair as though someone had set it on fire. He lunged for the red phone on the kitchen wall.

"What happened?" he demanded.

"Hines," Cait's voice whispered back, "I think. I don't know…. Oh, God, Sam, I just don't know."

His heart stopped. "Where?"

"In my kitchen."

Sam slammed down the telephone. Though it defied reason, he knew she'd know he hadn't hung up on her, that he was on his way.

He was out the door and standing on his balcony before he realized he was heading for his car in his boxer shorts. He swore and went back to his apartment. She needed him. And this time, damn it, *this* time he would do something about it. He wouldn't let her down.

He pulled on jeans and ran downstairs to the parking lot. It was a well-known fact that Maseratis needed to warm up when they'd been left cold for a while. Sam shot the transmission into drive and hit the road, the engine groaning and protesting.

When he got to her apartment, all the lights were on. He ran up the stairs and lifted his hand to knock, but the door opened before his fist could make contact with the wood. She stood there, pale and swaying a little, something white and sheer draping her body. She was alive, whole, unbloodied.

Sam didn't know what to do. He wanted to crush her to him and hold her. He wanted to beat the living daylights out of Hines. He wanted to find the man and tear him limb from limb. And he wanted Cait to do something besides stare at him as if she needed him desperately.

Because maybe he wouldn't be able to save the day for her this time, either.

"Where is he?" he asked hoarsely.

"I...don't know. He's gone now. If..." Cait trailed off miserably.

"You saw him?"

"I heard him."

Gradually, Sam's brain cleared. That, he thought, changed everything. "Maybe you were dreaming." But she'd called him, anyway, and that made his heart fill with something good.

Cait shook her head helplessly. She stepped back from the door.

Sam moved into her living room and looked

around. Nothing was disturbed. He went to the kitchen. It was spit-shined and perfect, not a chair or a utensil out of place. Then he heard her bare feet padding into the room behind him and he turned.

She might as well have been standing there naked. The nightgown was long and diaphanous, and every contour beneath it was outlined in the overhead fluorescent lights. All her flesh and curves. Nothing else. Sam felt something tighten into a hot knot inside him. She kept pushing him away. And now she stood here like this. Shaken, lost. Beautiful and damned near wearing nothing at all.

"Cait," he said hoarsely. "I have my limits."

"What?" she whispered, pressing knuckles to her mouth, her eyes still wild.

"What do you want from me, damn it?"

She lowered her hand slowly. "Make me sane again. Please. Make me whole."

He tried to hold on to himself while he wondered how he was supposed to do that without losing his mind. He tried not to look at her. "*Was* he here?"

"I don't know." Then she reached her hands out to him and he knew he was done.

For some reason his fingers always wanted to run through her hair. He went to her and let himself do it again, diving his fingers into all those fine, blond strands. It would have made sense to him if her hair had been long and flowing, wanton and free. But it was short and neat...and he loved messing it up.

He cupped her head and lowered his mouth to hers. He kissed her once. Neatly. Gently. Holding the last of himself back. "Are you okay?"

"No," she whispered.

"No?"

"Make it all go away."

Something inside him buckled. "You don't mean that. You've spent weeks telling me you don't."

"I was wrong. I changed my mind."

"There's a woman for you." He tried to joke, but his voice was a scrape in his throat.

"Sam, please, please touch me again."

It was what he'd wanted. But suddenly, in that moment, he knew that it wasn't going to cure him. He knew he wouldn't make love with her one more time and be able to walk away. If he did it even one more time, he'd be hers forever, body and soul.

He slid his hands up her hips, anyway, up her ribs, gathering the nightgown in his wake. She would protest, he thought, and that would be that. But then she folded her hands over his own and helped him. He drew breath and then the nightgown was over her head and puddled on the floor.

"You don't have to show me how this time, Sam."

Did she do that on purpose? Did she know the power she had?

There were parts of her he'd only just met before she'd locked them away, far from his touch, out of his reach. Now he rediscovered them, the dewy skin on the underside of her breasts, the hollow at her throat, the narrow waist. Sam tucked his hand beneath her knees and lifted her, because searching those places with his fingers again wasn't enough.

He carried her into the bedroom. The bed looked as though an animal had clawed its way free of the covers. And it was small. He hesitated.

"Don't stop now," she said. "One more time."

Once, from any other woman, those words would have comforted him. Now he heard denial rasp from his own throat. "For now."

She couldn't stand needing anymore, Cait thought. It had been something so big inside her for so long, ever since she had first touched him, growing wild and unruly after she'd kissed him again Monday night. She reached for him and pulled him down on top of her as he laid her on the bed.

But that wasn't what she wanted, either. She wanted his skin against her skin. She wanted to feel him inside her again.

She struggled with the snap on his jeans until he helped her. She groaned in protest when he eased away from her to pull his shirt over his head. He wore heart-patterned boxer shorts. She felt herself grinning, then laughing, until the sound hurt her chest. He was so good for her. So real. So unapologetically alive.

He leaned over her and caught her laugh with another kiss at the same time as he stripped off the hearts with the thumb of one hand. Then he had a moment of sanity.

"Cait, we can't keep doing this."

Something in her hazed brain tried to focus. She knew that, but she couldn't bear the truth now. Not now. "Don't."

"I mean, I'm not prepared for this again. How many chances can we take?"

She understood and something peaceful settled over her chest. There were no chances left to be had. She already had his child. "One more."

She arched up into him. His mouth sealed hers again. Then it traced hot and wet over her jaw, her collarbone, to her breast. His tongue tweaked her nipple, then he took it into his mouth, and things exploded inside her just as they had before.

She wrapped her legs around him and took him in. When she heard him groan her name, Cait smiled. For the second time in her life, she felt she was somewhere she belonged.

Eleven

Cait didn't think she would ever be able to move again. Her limbs felt languid, her mind empty, her heart sated. She rested her head against Sam's shoulder and made a sound that was half sigh, half moan.

Then, that quickly, she started shaking again.

She tried to ease away from him a little, knowing he would feel it. He caught her hip and tugged her back. "No, you don't."

"You don't even know what I was about to do," she protested, her voice husky and soft.

"You were going to regret."

Cait felt a little twitch go through her. She would, she knew, sooner or later, but not now. Eventually there would be no help for it. She couldn't let this go anywhere, not without telling him about the baby. And if she told him about the baby, that would change everything.

Anything that might have grown between them was already doomed, but she didn't regret what she had just done. If anything, it filled her with a fierce sense of exhilaration. She'd taken a bite out of life for herself. She'd grabbed something glorious, a memory that would last forever.

She couldn't explain any of that, so she told him

the truth, instead. "Sam, I think I'm losing my mind."

His chuckle was throaty, as though he, too, was drained from their lovemaking. "You? You're the sanest person I know."

"Not anymore." Something about her voice must have convinced him to let her go. He made no protest when she sat up. "I heard Branson Hines's voice in my kitchen."

She watched his face and wasn't sure if she was miserable or comforted when she saw doubt there. "What exactly did he say?"

"Does it matter?" She hugged her knees to her chest and wrapped her arms around them. "He wasn't really there."

"Tell me, anyway."

Cait thought about it. It was harder to remember than she might have expected. "I'm not sure about the beginning of it. I was asleep. I woke up to the sound of him. I was groggy."

"At the end, then." He rested a hand on her calf, and it was the most comforting feeling she had ever known.

"'Plan all you want,'" she repeated. "'You'll never get away from me.'"

Sam's brows rose. "Have you been planning anything?"

Cait flushed. So many things. None of them had anything directly to do with Hines. All her plans were about this man and the child she carried. But she *had* thought that leaving Mission Creek would help her escape from whoever was tormenting her.

Except...what if the only person who was tormenting her was herself? What if this was all in her mind?

"He said, 'You're mine,'" she whispered.

"Well, that's a crock. You're not."

"No."

"You're *mine*."

She wasn't prepared for the way her heart staggered or how much she wanted to believe him. She felt one corner of her mouth tug into a sad smile.

"Hey, hey," Sam said at her expression, sitting up, gathering her closer. "You're serious about this."

"That maybe I imagined it? Yes." But she let herself cling to him.

"Honey, that's ridiculous."

"I heard a man talking who wasn't there. I thought someone broke into my apartment because Billy got out. But what if he *did* dart out when I opened the door?"

"You said Billy doesn't do that," he reminded her.

"He's an animal. He's got whims. Nothing is carved in granite."

"You're missing one thing."

"The candle snuffer? They're delicate. I could have broken it myself."

But Sam shook his head. "Officer Needles said your kitchen doorknob had been scratched."

She cleaned a lot. Had she done that, too? She was just so grateful to finally have a place of her own. Had she tidied up the workbench downstairs? She couldn't remember anymore!

Agitated, she left the bed. She drove her fingers into her hair.

"Nice view," Sam said, grinning.

She looked down at herself, startled. She was naked—and she didn't even care. Part of it was that he felt as right in her world as her own skin. Part of it was that she was too terrified to fret over something so silly. "Sam, nothing was taken!" she blurted out.

He sobered as he realized that she was talking about her apartment again. "If the intent was to scare you, nothing would have been."

She'd never realized that he could be so patient, so pragmatic, so calm in the face of disaster. Then again, maybe she had. He'd been this way in the underground room, too. He'd held her together.

Now he was infuriating her because he refused to understand.

"There's no proof!" she declared hotly. "I want proof! I have nothing, Sam, nothing I can hold in my hand and say, see, this is real. This is truly happening. Maybe it's all like Jared said."

He tucked his chin. "Jared?"

Her damned tongue again, Cait thought. It had a mind of its own lately. She stared at him without answering, her heart slamming hard.

"Tell me about Jared," Sam suggested.

"No."

"Jared as in Cross?"

"There are several Jareds in the hospital."

"Not to my knowledge. And who mentioned the hospital?"

She couldn't defend her secrets when her mind was in shreds. "I saw him, okay? I went to him after what happened to us."

Sam laughed. "So did I."

Cait gaped at him. "You did? Why?"

"Because I couldn't get you off my mind. I thought he could fix me. He failed spectacularly."

Her legs crumpled. Cait sat where she stood. "Don't say that."

"You asked. Why did *you* go to him?"

"Because I was feeling...out of sorts."

"Mentally?" He circled his index finger at his temple. "Or because you still wanted me, too?"

"Stop it! Will you just stop and take this seriously?"

Sam sobered. "Cait, I will very rarely do that in my life. I'm sorry."

He seemed to be saying so much more than she meant, but she let it go. "He said I might dream," she said hoarsely.

"And you think tonight was a dream?"

"It started while I was sleeping."

"Were you sleepwalking in your kitchen before you called me?"

"No."

"Then that part wasn't a dream. Did you hear him then?"

She had, she remembered. But did that mean anything? She'd thought she'd seen the note when she was wide awake, too. "I can't even prove *that* was real. I flushed it away."

She felt a tremor go through her as soon as she heard her own words. The room felt cold, then hot. She wanted to reach out with her hand and snatch them back.

"What?" he asked almost too quietly. "You flushed what?"

"Just something else I imagined."

"Imagined how, where, when and in what context?"

Oh, yes, she thought, his joie de vivre hid a steel-trap mind. He took nothing seriously—he was right about that—except the things that mattered.

She had a sickening sense of doors closing on her, trapping her with her own evasions. Then she remembered something another child had taught her once in one of the foster homes. When you lie, keep it as close to the truth as possible. Then you're not as likely to screw it up.

She was going to lose Sam, anyway. Sooner or later. But not now, here, tonight. She couldn't bear it. She would tell him about the note, but not what it had said.

"I found a piece of paper in my locker, at the hospital. Something was written on it."

"What?"

"It was just a vague threat. I don't know. I was shaken up. I don't remember." She covered her eyes with a hand, every pore, every cell in her body caught in an agony of shame and regret for the lie.

"And you flushed it away?"

Cait nodded. Then, when she looked up again, she lost her breath for a moment. He was furious.

"Why the hell didn't you tell me this?" he demanded.

"Because it's my problem."

"And you're *my* problem."

"Thank you very much."

"Damn it, don't twist my words."

"I think they speak for themselves."

"You know what I mean."

"No, Sam, I really don't."

"You were mine to protect and I didn't."

"You saved my life in that room!" She screamed it. She had never known she was capable of screaming before. Her words bounced off the walls, then she realized she was crying again. "You kept me alive," she whispered, her voice breaking and softening. "You were exactly what I needed. Are you crazy? If you had acted like some kind of madman, if you had tried to beat Hines up or gotten shot, I would never have had a sane thought again in my life. Instead, you were clever and steady. You didn't let me climb up into the pipes in the ceiling."

"Cait…" He stared at her.

"Why is that so hard for you to believe?" she continued desperately. "Where do men get the idea that they have to throw punches to be a hero? You used your mind."

"It didn't work."

"It did. Oh, Sam, it did," she said wretchedly. "You placated Hines, kept him calm, until we were rescued. If you hadn't been there, he would have killed me. He was vibrating like a piano wire, and I would have done something stupid to set him off."

She saw something new come into Sam's eyes. Something curious and inward turning. Something she knew he hadn't bumped up against before. He'd never realized any of this before.

But he was considering it. She could give him that at least, before this was all over.

She wanted desperately to touch him. She fisted her hands together in her lap, instead, and then she wondered why. Why couldn't she touch him again? Why couldn't she reach out to him?

One more time.

Cait stood up shakily. This time she wasn't trying to hide from the nightmare. This time she wasn't searching desperately for something to ground her and bring her back to herself. This time she was calm. She crossed to the bed. He looked at her, startled, then he smiled slowly as his eyes raked up and down her nakedness again.

"You're my hero," she said quietly.

He reached for her fast, tumbling her down on top of him again.

She straddled him, then braced herself on her hands and knees above him. She did the things he had done to her a short while ago. Because they had felt good and they had made her shiver. She had nothing else to go on.

She ran her tongue under the lobe of his ear, down his throat. She thought she heard him groan, but her blood was pounding in her ears and she couldn't be sure. She nipped at his chin until he caught her face in his hands and kissed her. She teased his tongue for a moment, then she pulled away to trail butterfly kisses down his chest. His fingers dug into her hair.

She felt energized, empowered, brazen. She lowered herself on him and felt him hard against her and was amazed that he could respond that fast, that sure, for her. Then she shifted her weight and took him inside her.

This time she was the one who cried out his name.

By morning Cait realized that Sam was perfectly willing and able to hold a grudge. When she got out of the shower, she heard him banging things around in her kitchen.

Something shook deep at the core of her over the night they had shared and the fact that he had stayed. Somehow she had never expected him to stay the night, to sleep beside her. Well, on top of her. Her bed had never been meant for two. But they'd fit together just fine.

It made her ache. It made her yearn for more in a way she had not allowed herself to do in a very long time. But now...now he was angry.

"You didn't trust me," he said, slamming the door on the microwave hard.

"You're naked," she said to change the subject. Then she smiled. There was a gorgeous, naked man in her kitchen and he'd spent the night loving her.

"I wanted coffee. Most American households have coffee. It was an immediate need, so I didn't bother to get dressed first."

Cait nodded as though that made all the sense in the world. "You can have the shower now."

"I don't want a shower. I want coffee."

"I don't have any."

"I know that."

"Stop being cranky. You found the tea bags." He held one in his hand.

"Real men don't drink tea."

"Real men smell better after a shower."

The microwave beeped and he reached in for the cup. It was hot and he swore and snatched his hand back to suck on his thumb. "Damn it, Cait, you didn't trust me."

Cait flinched inwardly. "I trusted you a great deal. I gave you all of me."

Something flared in his eyes. "You know what I mean. You didn't tell me about the note."

Something cold settled inside her. "I didn't tell *anyone* about it."

"Why not? That makes no damned sense."

She scrambled. "Seriously, Sam, who was I going to tell?"

"Me. The police. You're being threatened."

"It scared me and I panicked. I flushed it." She paused, getting a grip on herself. "I couldn't go to the cops after that because I was afraid it would sound like some cockamamie story I made up." Oh, the lie was bitter on her tongue. "And I told you the first chance I got."

His eyes narrowed on her. "Well, we're telling the police now. I just called Jake White."

Cait gaped at him. "It's six o'clock in the morning."

"I know. The desk sergeant had to wake him up at home to give him my message."

Cait groaned. Tabitha was going to kill her. Then again, Tabitha was used to cops. Her father had been one.

"He just called me back," Sam continued, "While you were in the shower. We're meeting him at the police station at eight o'clock."

"We're supposed to be at the hospital at eight o'clock."

"I called there, too, and told them we'd be late."

Cait nodded, then the impact of his words rolled

over her, robbing her of breath. "Jake called you back *here?*"

He looked at her oddly. "I didn't think to grab my cell phone when I raced out of my condo last night to come here. How else was he supposed to get in touch with me?"

"Jake called you back *here?*" she squealed again.

"Honey, you're repeating yourself."

"Then he knows you spent the night here."

Sam appeared to think about it. "Well, yeah. I guess."

Cait felt everything inside her fall apart. If Jake knew, then Tabitha knew. And...

Who cared?

She realized, with a heartache that pushed tears into her eyes, that it really didn't matter anymore. Her privacy was shredded, but she wouldn't be in Mission Creek long enough for it to make a difference. And that hurt more, far more, than the idea of anyone whispering about her behind her back.

"I'm a Sam Walters woman," she whispered.

"Honey, you're a lot more than that."

Things rocked inside her. She wanted to tell him again not to say such things, yet she couldn't find the breath. "I'm going to go get dressed." She clutched her towel a little more tightly around her.

"Don't do it on my account."

She glanced back at him, then she turned and threw herself at him. One more time.

Sam caught her and kissed her. He started aiming her back toward the bedroom. "I like the way your mind works. I hate tea, anyway."

"Mm."

"But, honey," he said as he lowered himself on top of her, "we've really got to rethink this bed."

They were silent on the drive to the police station. Cait looked drained. Sam felt overwhelmed. How much more was he supposed to have her before he got over her? Where was that itchy feeling, that sense of panic, the need to escape? It was buried, he thought, beneath a fear for her that nearly left him emasculated.

He parked in the municipal lot beside the police station. It was crowded because officers were gathered for morning roll call. He found himself taking her elbow as they went inside. Protecting her. Because he knew if he lost her now, if anything happened to her, he would die.

His sense of urgency and desperation built as they made their way down the corridor to Jake White's office. If the man was interested in what had transpired between them last night, it didn't show. He was drinking from a mug, and the room smelled like coffee. He opened his mouth to greet them, but Sam cut him off.

"Is that caffeine?" He nodded at Jake's mug. "Real caffeine?"

Jake peered down at the liquid. "In some societies, cop shops being one."

"Can I have some?"

"There's the pot right there in the corner. Use the knife beside it if you need to jar the stuff loose."

Sam poured a cup and drank it black, grinning. "Nectar of the gods."

Jake lifted a brow. "You're either hungover or

otherwise in a bad way.'' He motioned to the chairs in front of his desk. "So tell me what's been going on.''

Cait sat quickly. Her voice faltered a little as she told him about hearing Hines's voice in her kitchen. She got breathless when she tried to skim over the issue of the note.

"What did it say?'' Jake asked sharply, jotting on a legal pad.

"I don't remember,'' Cait said hollowly.

"You don't remember?''

Sam interjected then and made her feel painfully small. "She panicked and threw it out right away.''

Jake looked skeptical. "Where? Can we get it back? It could have prints on it. There weren't any on the candle snuffer. For that matter, we might be able to do something with the handwriting.''

"She flushed it,'' Sam said. "Look, this obviously has something to do with Branson Hines.''

Jake scowled and sat back in his chair. "Not so obviously.''

"Who the hell else would want to hurt her?''

Jake glanced at Cait. "That was my next question. Do you have any enemies?''

She felt vaguely embarrassed. "I never let myself get close enough to anyone to make enemies.''

Jake glanced between her and Sam, then he finally nodded. "Okay, here's my problem. I can't for the life of me figure out how Hines could have been in your kitchen last night when he's in prison this morning.''

"You're sure of that?'' Sam asked harshly.

"Beyond a doubt. I just spoke to the man myself.''

"You called him?" Cait asked, startled.

"I called the warden and had him rouse Hines out of his cell and put him on the phone so I could hear his voice."

"This makes no damned sense, then," Sam growled.

"Tell me about it," Jake agreed. "One other thing does occur to me. What with you two being an item now and all."

An item? Cait felt herself flush. "We're not...I don't..."

Jake didn't give her a chance to finish. "How can I put this delicately?" he asked. "You've had other items," he said to Sam.

Cait felt her skin flame. Another Sam Walters woman. But, God help her, it hadn't felt like that last night.

"Think any of your exes are ticked off?" Jake asked.

Sam sat back as though the thought stunned him. "Enough to go after Cait?"

"Think about it. I don't want a knee-jerk answer. I want you to dwell on it and see if any personalities come to mind that might fit this."

Cait risked a glance at him. He looked murderous. "I will."

"Well, then." Jake stood. "I'll walk you back out to your car."

Cait got to her feet quickly, as well. "That's all?"

"Without concrete physical proof, all I can do is trace down a few ideas. See if they pan out."

It was more or less what she had thought last night. "I'm sorry we wasted your time."

Jake looked startled. "You didn't. Someone's harassing you. It's my job to figure out who." They were in the parking lot before he added, "By the way, my wife-to-be advises me that if I don't corner you two into going out with us this weekend, I'm not welcome over her threshold anytime in the foreseeable future."

"Sure," Sam said easily. "What about Friday night?"

Cait felt her heart hurtle. She was going to Laredo on Friday. "I—"

"I'll clear it with Tabitha and call you," Jake said.

She couldn't keep doing this! Last night was one thing. She'd been scared and she'd called her hero. But Friday? Friday her new life started. "I—" she began again.

Sam opened the car door for her. "Cait likes Tex-Mex. A lot."

"No, I—"

"Coyote Harry's, then? Good. Sounds like a plan to me. They have a band there on weekends after nine o'clock."

The car door shut on Cait as she slid onto the seat, trapping her inside. She pressed her hands to her cheeks.

She told herself there was no way she could politely refuse. But she knew in her heart that she didn't want to. She glanced at Sam as he got behind the wheel. She wanted to have dinner with him Friday night. And Saturday night. She wanted to have breakfast with him Sunday morning.

She was in love with him.

* * *

The woman watched them from a car parked on the street in front of the police station. Her gaze lingered on Jake White, then it danced to Cait, then to Sam, as they got into his car. Her anger seethed.

It had been such a small kernel at first, at the very heart of her, back when this had started. But day by day, it mushroomed into something uglier and more treacherous. The betrayal ate at her. The unfairness of it all clawed at her soul. Now, watching the three of them together, she wanted to scream.

They were thicker than thieves, she thought. And each one of them was, in some way, responsible for destroying her.

She wanted to destroy each of them in return, wanted to take a piece out of each of them that would hurt them badly. Oh, yes, she would end up with Cait's baby. The little nurse was obviously rattled, proving the game last night had worked. But that wasn't enough anymore. Now the woman knew that she couldn't leave until every one of them knew what it was to lose everything.

She put her car in gear and slid away from the curb before Sam's car could pass hers and one of them could recognize her.

Twelve

Molly Gates had never forgotten Caitlyn Matthews. Over a year ago, when Molly had thought that her career with the Mission Creek Police Department was unraveling faster than she could catch the threads, when she'd first begun to suspect that there were a lot of bad cops in town with an agenda of their own, Caitlyn had saved the day for her. Unwittingly, of course, but she'd done it. When the Lion's Den, the network of twisted police officers, had beaten up a teenage boy to teach him a lesson, Cait had gone out of her way to make sure the boy got good care, with or without health insurance. And she had been with Bobby Jansen when Bobby had startled babbling incoherently about the cop ring. It would have been easy for Cait to have dismissed everything he'd said as delusional ramblings, as Molly herself almost had. It would have been second nature for most people not to have gotten involved in such an ugly situation. But Cait had made it a point to tell Molly everything Bobby had said.

And then, finally, the pieces of the Lion's Den had all started clicking together for her. Molly had come out of the mess with her gold detective's shield and a man she loved more than sense. And by Molly's staunch, backstreet code, that meant she owed the Mission Creek Memorial nurse a debt of gratitude.

"So what's your take on it?" Molly asked Jake White, lifting the coffeepot from its hot plate in the corner of his office. She sniffed its contents. "Ugh."

Jake watched her, chewing his lip. "You know, I heard a rumor that you once ate a piece of day-old pizza in that task-force war room when you were breaking the Lion's Den."

Molly glanced at him. "I was proving a point."

"Well, my coffee can't be worse than that."

"Five bucks says that it is." But she poured some, anyway. "Caitlyn Matthews," she said again, moving to sit in front of his desk. "Tell me what you think of all this, then tell me what I can do to help."

Jake thought about it. "Tabitha knows her a lot better than I do—which is to say not much at all. But she feels that if Ms. Matthews is imagining this, then the sun rises at night."

Molly nodded her understanding. "Not possible unless the apocalypse is on its way."

"That's about the size of it. There's not a doubt in Tabitha's mind that someone broke into Ms. Matthews's apartment, someone left her a nasty note, and someone made like Branson Hines in her kitchen last night."

Molly leaned back and stretched out her jeans-clad legs. She loved being a detective and out of uniform. "That last part is particularly nasty, if you ask me."

"Considering what all she went through a few weeks ago, yes, indeed."

"So it either really is Hines, or someone hates her a very great deal."

"To do something like that? I agree. But Hines is in jail."

Molly nodded. "So the next question is, who hates that nice, pretty nurse?"

"She says she has no enemies."

"They all say that." Molly stood again to pace. "Think I can I have a look-see around her apartment? That might tell us something."

"It was going to be my next step. Hold on. I'll see if I can arrange it." Jake picked up the phone and called the hospital. He asked for his fiancée, who promptly put him on hold. Molly could tell from the tone of the conversation that Cait Matthews was the next one to come on the line. Then Jake put *her* on hold.

"When do you want to do it?" he asked Molly.

She glanced at her watch. "I have an appointment tonight that I can't break. The director of the rec center where I volunteer is receiving a commendation from the city. Big hoopla. I'm even wearing a dress." And that, she thought, would knock her husband's eyes out. She grinned privately. "How about first thing in the morning? Say eight o'clock."

Jake picked up the phone again and arranged it with Cait. "I'll take a run over to Laredo tomorrow, too," he said when he hung up. "We're taking it for granted that Deena is in that flophouse Hines keeps calling, but I want to see her with my own eyes and have a word with her."

"She wasn't implicated in anything Hines did, so we can't exactly spend tax dollars or violate her civil rights by keeping tabs on her."

"Bingo. But if Hines is reaching out for Caitlyn

Matthews from his jail cell, then who better to use than his missus?''

Molly started to agree, then shook her head. "You know what bothers me? Of all the people Hines might have developed a grudge against through all that, why Caitlyn Matthews? Others had a bigger part in bringing him down. All she did was escape.''

Jake stood from his desk. "Maybe she tweaked his antennae somehow.''

"I just don't see it.''

"Yeah, it bothers me, too. Which is why I want Sam Walters to think a little about who *he* might have ticked off lately. This has the ring of a jealous lover.''

"We'll get to the bottom of it,'' Molly assured him. "Just as soon as I go flash my legs at Danny.''

Jake laughed. "Lucky man.''

"You don't know the half of it.''

Cait hung up the phone in Tabitha's office and watched her Friday excursion to Laredo run through her fingers like sand. Then again, Sam probably wouldn't have left her side long enough for her to make the drive, anyway. He'd been sticking to her like glue all day.

She looked at Tabitha, who'd called Cait to her private office for Jake's call.

"He's sending someone to look at my apartment tomorrow morning,'' Cait explained. "Molly Gates. I know her.''

"The one who asked you to look in on Beatty Jansen?''

"That's the one.''

"She can't do it today?"

"Apparently not. I'd already put in for a sick day tomorrow, anyway. I was…" Cait trailed off. "I was going to do some errands," she said feebly.

Tabitha cocked her head. "It's not like you to take a day off for something like that. Tell me the truth. You're secretly running off for a long dirty weekend with Sam, right?"

Cait's breath caught in her throat and she coughed. "Where do you get these ideas?"

"I'm not passing judgment," Tabitha said. "I think it's great."

"I'm doing errands."

"If that's what they call it these days." Tabitha shrugged. "I just find it very interesting that Sam also canceled our double-date dinner tomorrow night."

Cait's heart sank. It was the first she'd heard of it. "He did?" He'd lost interest in her already. She'd known he would, sooner or later, but it hit her like a wrecking ball.

"He didn't tell you?" Tabitha's eyes narrowed. "He changed it to Saturday night."

"I haven't really spoken to him." Cait almost had to spit out the lie this time. Yes, she was definitely getting back to herself.

"He said you guys had another engagement. You're meeting his parents."

"I'm *what?*"

But Tabitha was gone again, in the outer office conferring with her assistant.

Cait took two, then three deep, steadying breaths. It didn't work. It didn't calm her. Panic clawed along her nerve endings. She couldn't meet his parents. She couldn't get in that deep. She couldn't bear to enjoy his family, too, then let it all go.

She went to find Sam. He was in his office and his door was open. She barged in and slammed it shut behind her, leaning her back against it. "I'm not meeting your parents."

He looked up, surprised. Then he settled back in his chair. "It's their wedding anniversary. I completely forgot about it until my sister called me this morning. Big bash at their house. And I'm *not* going alone."

"I'm not getting involved with your family!" It would complicate everything. "I'm...I'm..."

Sam waited.

"A one-time thing!" she blurted.

"Honey, we're pushing five now. Or is it six?"

"Stop it!"

"All right. But you're still my date for tomorrow night."

He was teasing her, but she couldn't get her equilibrium together enough to joust back. Which terrified her. "I have errands," she pleaded. "I can't."

"You have errands during the day. We're not going to the party until seven o'clock. Besides, I'm doing those errands with you."

"But you have to work."

"I'll be on call. I switched with another doctor."

"You can't do this!"

"What? Watch over you? Protect you?"

"It was all in my mind!"

"When Jake White tells me that, I'll believe it."

Cait felt something shift inside her and it almost broke her heart. "Sam," she said softly, "you don't have to do this. Nothing that happened with Hines was your fault.''

''I know.''

''You do?''

''I've come to realize that, now that you've knocked me over the head with it a few times. I'm watching over you now because I can't lose you.''

She felt her breath catch and her eyes fill. How had this all gotten so complicated?

Cait turned to flee the room. His voice stopped her again. ''By the way, we're staying at my condo tonight. I can't take that bed of yours even one more time.''

She hesitated, then left, slamming the door behind her.

Sam waited until he was sure she was gone, then picked up the telephone to check that the cleaning service was at his condo. They were supposed to be—it was Thursday. But he was about to bring a woman to his condo for the first time in his life, and he wanted to make sure.

By the sheer grace of the Hippocratic Oath, Cait managed to race back to her apartment by herself the next morning. Sam was called to the hospital whether he liked it or not. She was reasonably sure that the only reason he hadn't argued with her about making the appointment with Molly later was that the woman was a police detective.

As Cait made the quick drive, part of her had a sweet ache. She still felt overwhelmed by what was happening to her life. Sam had spent the night touching her as though he really meant something by it.

She met Molly in front of her garage at five past eight. She jumped out of her car, saying, "I'm sorry I'm late."

Molly grinned. "If he's a good man, then it was worth my time."

Cait flushed. "I'm not…he's not…"

"Save it for someone who hasn't been there. For now, I want you to walk me through this whole business of Hines's voice. Okay?"

"Yes. Yes, of course."

Cait hightailed it for the stairs. She let the detective in, and for the next ten minutes she explained in detail what had happened. At first she felt like a fool. Each time she recited the story, she thought she sounded more and more like a raving lunatic. She'd had a dream and had come undone. Or, heaven help her, she was hearing voices that weren't there. Then it struck her that she actually trusted this woman. If Molly Gates thought this was purely a product of her imagination, then Cait had no doubt she would just come out and tell her so. There was something basic about the woman, some rough times just shading the corners of her eyes. Cait sensed they shared a common past. She guessed that Molly Gates had come by what she had the hard way, just as Cait had.

In all her life, she had never trusted anyone. And now there was Sam and Tabitha and this woman. Her life was getting crowded. She didn't know whether to laugh at that or to cry.

"Well?" she asked finally when she'd finished her story.

"Hold on," Molly said. Then she started rummaging through her kitchen.

Twenty minutes later, when the cabinets, cupboards and refrigerator yielded nothing interesting, the last thing she did was open the kitchen door that led down to the garage. "Ah. Here's your answer. Grab me a kitchen towel, will you?"

"What?" Cait demanded, but she obediently grabbed a towel from a drawer and handed it to her.

Molly used it to pick something up off the top step. "How about a box?" she asked, instead of replying. "A shoe box or something. Do you have anything like that handy?"

"I don't know. Let me look."

Cait found one in her bedroom closet—it had held the high heels she'd bought for the ball. She hurried back to the kitchen with it and watched as Molly deposited a small tape player in it. Then she stuck her finger in the towel and used that to hit a button.

In the next instant, Hines's voice filled the room again. Cait gasped and flinched.

"Easy," Molly said. "It's just newfangled electronics."

"Someone taped his voice?" She was disbelieving. She needed to sit down.

Molly nodded. "I'm going to take this back to the station to see what we can find out by examining the tape itself. It's our stroke of luck that no one's had a chance to reclaim this little toy yet."

"Someone taped his voice," Cait said again, amazed.

Molly's expression softened. "Caitlyn, you have an enemy. Someone who knew the one thing that would come closest to striking your soul."

"I have an enemy," she whispered. It was all too much.

"Who?" Molly pressed.

Misery flooded her. "I don't know."

"Well, then," Molly said, "I guess we're going to have to go about this with forensic expertise. We'll see if we can lift any prints off this gadget." She picked the box up again and started out of the kitchen.

Cait's mind locked on one thing. "I didn't imagine it," she said.

Molly hesitated and glanced back. "Everything that's been happening to you? Nope."

"I'm not crazy."

Molly grinned. "Not to hear anyone who knows you tell it."

Cait stood on unsteady legs and went with the detective into the living room to see her out. She wasn't crazy. Now she could go about making some sense of the rest of the mess of her life.

And what a mess it was, she thought at a quarter past seven that evening. Sam eased the Maserati to a stop in front of a sprawling split level in a pleasant part of town. Cars already spilled out of the driveway. Lights glittered in every window. Looking at it, Cait felt overwhelmed. How could she do this?

She still wasn't sure why she had allowed Sam to drag her here. For that matter, she wasn't sure why she hadn't gone to Laredo today after Molly Gates had left her apartment. She could have escaped undetected while Sam was at the hospital. In truth, Cait realized she didn't know much of anything anymore, except that someone really was after her and she wasn't out of her mind. And she couldn't bear to waste these precious days when Sam seemed to want her.

"Brace yourself," he said, coming around to open her door.

Cait swung her feet to the pavement and stood. "For what?"

"Noise and misery."

"I don't understand." She followed him up the walkway.

"All but one of my siblings has been married so many times there's a total of fifteen kids among them. And my parents wish they'd never gotten married at all."

"But they're still together," she said, joining him at the door.

"Forty-five years tonight."

"Why?"

He looked at her as though she had spoken in Chinese.

"If they wish they hadn't gotten married," she persisted, "why would they stay together forty-five years?"

"Inertia, probably." He opened the door.

A wall of sound hit Cait and almost knocked her over. Shrieks and laughter. Shouts and music. There were people everywhere. She remembered what he had said before regarding his parents' life. "This isn't boring," she murmured, stepping inside.

An older woman swept down on them. Cait had a bad moment when she thought she was aiming at her.

But she went for Sam, clutching his face in her hands. "Sammy."

"Sammy?" Cait echoed.

He glanced at her out of the corner of his eye. "Breathe a word of that and you die."

"Might be worth it."

"Cait, I'm serious—"

"And who's this?" the woman interrupted.

"Cait Matthews," Sam said. "My mother, Maribel Walters."

Maribel looked back at Sam, clearly astounded. "You brought a woman?" Then she turned back to the room and clapped her hands. "Listen up, everyone. Sammy brought a woman!"

Cait wished the floor would open beneath her feet and swallow her. Then she fully registered Maribel Walters's words and her world swung out of orbit again. Sam went through the female hospital staff like a hungry man at a smorgasbord. Hadn't he ever brought one of those women home?

She looked at him. She wanted to know. She *needed* to know. What did this mean? But then a young woman thrust a plate of little sandwich pieces into her hand.

"I'm Sandy," she said.

"Hello. I'm Cait."

"I know. Mom told me. I'm Sam's sister."

"I'm pleased to meet you." Cait still hadn't gotten much more than three feet into the house, and now Sandy was circling her.

"What's the matter?" Cait asked. Was she overdressed? Underdressed? She looked down at herself.

With the state of her mind these days, had she forgotten to put clothes on entirely?

"She's got all her limbs, Sammy," Sandy said to her brother. "So you didn't bring her home out of pity."

"I'm whole, thank you." Cait took a quick bite of a sandwich.

"Cute, too," said Sandy. Then she was off again.

Cait lost Sam. One minute he was there, then he was absorbed into the chaos. She panicked for a brief moment, then forced herself to relax. She ate and looked around, greedily taking in all this…family.

Another woman sidled up to her. "Hi, I'm Traci." She held out a hand.

Cait moved her sandwich plate to shake hands with her. "Hi. Another sister?"

"Yup. I'm the baby of the family." Her eyes coasted up and down Cait.

Cait had had time to think of a defense against all these questions. "Sam only brought me because he feels responsible for me," she explained.

To her amazement, the woman laughed. "Sam feels responsible for no one."

"Patients," Cait corrected.

"Well, that's true."

"And we were kidnapped together."

"So he's going to marry you to make up for that?" Traci laughed again. "Not our Sammy."

Traci moved away. Cait spied an open space on a settee and moved that way, lowering herself gently before her legs could give out. *Marry* her?

A child landed at her feet. "Hi. I'm Lucas."

Cait found her voice yet again. Here was comfortable ground. She was good with kids. "Hi yourself. I'm Cait."

"I know. Everybody said. Isn't this fun? I love coming to Gram's house."

"I can understand why."

"It's not always like this, though," Lucas confided. "Only when everyone comes."

"Does that happen often?"

"As often as Mom can arrange it," another woman said, sitting down beside Cait. "She lives for this stuff. I'm Abigail. Spare your voice. I already know. You're Cait and you got kidnapped with Sammy. Would you like a drink?"

"Um, no, thanks." She was parched, but she couldn't drink liquor.

"Here," Sam said, appearing in front of her, holding out a glass of milk.

Something in her heart rolled over. Cait took the glass. "Thank you."

"Leave her alone, Abby," Sam said. "She doesn't need to hear tales of my misspent youth." Then he was off again, laughing with a dark-haired man in one corner of the room. The boy, Lucas, got up and scampered off, as well.

Cait put her plate and her milk down beside the settee and hunted for a washroom. She found a powder room down a short corridor beside the rec room, knocking twice to make sure no one was inside. There were so many people here, it boggled her mind. When there was no answer to her knock, she slipped into the room and just stood, collecting her breath.

Then she looked in the mirror and was amazed to find tears glinting in her eyes.

Hormones, she thought wildly. That was all it was. She wasn't crazy. Molly Gates had proved that someone really was after her, so she wasn't nuts. And not once, she thought, not once since that revelation, had she truly felt fear. Because the only thing that really terrified her was becoming a stranger to herself. And losing her child.

If she wasn't crazy, no one would take her baby. If all this wasn't in her mind, then she was safe. Sam wouldn't let anything happen to her.

Cait stared at herself. She saw rosy cheeks, despite her exhaustion from all her sleepless nights lately. The face that looked back at her wore a lopsided grin. She was safe, because for the first time in her life she wasn't alone.

Maybe Sam would leave her when this was over. But for now someone hated her enough to try to drive her insane, and he was standing by her. Her world had been turned upside down, but now, for this pure, special place in time, she had everything.

Cait opened the door to slip back out of the bathroom and ran into Sam's chest.

"Are you all right?" he asked her.

She pulled back a little. "Perfect."

"You're enjoying this?"

Never, not once in her whole life, had she been included in a family like this. "I'm loving it."

He stared at her in surprise for a moment. "We'll go soon. I just needed to put in an appearance."

"No."

He eased her back into the light of the powder room to look down at her face. "You're serious."

"Do you even know what you have here?"

"Mass chaos and tribal warfare."

She punched his chest.

"Wrong answer?" he asked.

"Family. Oh, it is so precious. You don't understand, Sam, because you've always had it."

Then they heard footsteps coming along the hall outside, punctuated by whispers.

Sam stepped into the room with her. He eased the door shut behind him, and they stood close together in the tiny space. "I think someone wants a moment alone," he whispered.

"You?"

"Me, too." He closed his mouth over hers.

Cait wasn't sure she could hold so much happiness. And in that moment she knew it was going to cripple her to let it all go. Then he pulled back and touched a finger to her lips. "Shh." He reached and turned the light out.

"What are you doing?" For a wild moment she thought he might be considering making love with her pressed up against the wall. Then he turned around and eased the door open again a crack.

Maribel Walters was standing there, just outside the door, with a gray-haired man Cait hadn't met yet. Sam's father, Cait guessed instinctively. And in a gesture that struck Cait to her soul, the man put his fingers to the woman's lips much as Sam had just done to her.

"Thank you," the man said to Maribel. "Thank you for always being my best friend."

Maribel Walters snaked her arms around his neck and held him close. "You're welcome, you old fool. Happy anniversary."

Thirteen

Tabitha went with Jake to Laredo on Saturday morning. Neither of them expected much to come of his visit to the motel, but they could have lunch in the city afterward and she figured she could do a little shopping. During the drive, they dissected Cait's life with all the glee of two gossipmonger cronies, trying to make sense of what was happening to her.

"The tape's real, but spliced," Jake explained. "It's Hines, all right, but pieces of it have been omitted. Someone else was probably talking in those missing sections."

"The person who's doing this to her?" Tabitha asked.

"Good guess."

"How could they manage such a thing?"

"Call him in jail and tape the conversation. There's deep static on the tape, too. Our experts think it comes from lifting the conversation off a phone line."

"And you still think it's one of Sam's ditched dates?"

"That makes the most sense. Get Cait out of the picture and maybe lure Sam back?"

"Get her out of the picture by putting her in a loony bin," Tabitha clarified.

"Or by unraveling her so much that Sam no longer finds her interesting."

"He's amazing me," Tabitha said.

"How so?"

"There's a pool going on at the hospital. Five-dollar buy-in, guessing how long it's going to be before he moves on. He's never dated the same woman more than a few times."

Jake grinned. "What's your bet?"

"That he doesn't move on."

Jake lifted a brow at her. "No kidding. Are you serious?"

Tabitha sat back more comfortably in her seat. "It's Mission Creek Memorial," she explained. "And for some reason, love has really been in the air there lately."

Gil Travalini was released from the hospital on Saturday morning. Cait wanted to be there to see him off. Her stomach also felt delicate and she did not want to be at Sam's condo in the event she suffered another bout of morning sickness. How would she explain it?

Her lies were building, stretching out, like a row of dominoes. And she knew, sooner or later, that one of them was going to fall, sending all the others into collapse. She stood in Sam's bathroom and closed her eyes against the mental image, willing her stomach to settle.

"Please," she whispered aloud. "Not yet. Just let me get out of here."

She had to do something about her life.

How could she be so happy and so miserable at

the same time? Because, she answered herself, life was precious and sweet right now, but she was going to lose it all. She couldn't continue this way indefinitely.

Last night, after they'd left the powder room, Cait had stood in the kitchen of Sam's parents' home and had known that she was going to have to tell him about the baby. The sure knowledge had rolled over her all at once, robbing her of breath so completely that Sam had thought she was ill, or at least exhausted by everything that had been happening lately. He'd whisked her out of there. But that hadn't put the truth out of her mind.

And once she told him it everything would change, end, fracture. It would upset this delicate balance between them. She had no idea how he would react, but she did know that nothing would ever be the same between them again.

At least, she thought, she'd had this precious time with him, a golden spot of weeks that she would remember all her life. At least she could tell this child that she'd loved his or her father completely.

Cait realized she was shaking just as Sam's voice came through the bathroom door. "Are you all right, or are you just taking up residence in there?"

"No, I'm...I'm done." She wrapped a towel around herself and stepped out of the room.

He'd left the bedroom. Cait dressed hurriedly and found him in the kitchen. He was at the table, looking at a photo album. "What's that?" she asked.

"One of life's last great mysteries." He took a swig from a mug of coffee.

Cait went to look over his shoulder. "Is that your parents' wedding?"

He didn't answer right away. He'd been quiet all through their drive home last night, too, and through most of the night and morning. "Yeah. I've wondered my entire life why they stayed together when there was no fun, no laughter."

Cait hugged herself. "Life is more than fun and laughter."

"That occurred to me while we were spying on them last night."

She held her breath, not sure where this was going but sensing it was important.

"I always thought they were bored and miserable together," he continued finally.

Cait sighed. "That wasn't boredom we saw, Sam. That was peace."

He looked over his shoulder at her. "How did you get to be so smart?"

She wanted to smile and couldn't quite pull it off. "It's always easiest to recognize something from a distance."

"Forests and trees?"

She nodded. "I spent a lifetime watching other people have it. Outside, looking in."

"Ah, honey."

He reached to take her hand, but Cait stepped away. The words *it's over* were a booming litany in her head now. Sometime today she would tell him. "I've got to get dressed."

"I'm going with you to the hospital."

"You don't have—"

"Yes. I do."

She didn't argue. She had so little time with him left.

Gilbert was glad to be going home, yet shaken at the thought of leaving behind all the people he'd grown close to during his extended stay in the hospital. Cait had seen it a hundred times, which was why she wanted to be here for him when he left.

She stayed with him until he climbed into his wheelchair, clutching teddy bears and balloons. Then she gave him one last hug and gently disengaged herself from him before he was taken downstairs to the lobby. She knew that if she watched him wheeled out the front doors of the hospital, she'd get misty-eyed. She didn't want to do that to him. This was emotional enough for the boy as it was.

Besides, Sam would be with him all the way.

"Where are you going?" Sam asked as she stepped away.

"I thought I'd run downstairs for a cup of tea." She held up one of the decaffeinated tea bags she'd taken to carting around in her purse. "Your condo is seriously lacking in my favorite amenities."

A grin touched one corner of his mouth. "Now you know how it feels. We'll stop at the store and pick up some of the things you like on the way home from here."

She felt as if her whole body spasmed, but he didn't seem to notice. "I've got to go."

By the time she reached the cafeteria, her heart felt wooden. She got hot water for her tea and went to a table, praying that no one saw fit to join her. She needed to think.

Once, she thought a little giddily, the idea of anyone taking it upon themselves to sit down with her
would have been so farfetched as to be ludicrous. It
was just a measure of how far her life had come since
her abduction…and how far it had yet to go.

What was she going to do now?

She couldn't leave Mission Creek, she realized,
any more than she could continue to hide the truth
from Sam. She couldn't do it to escape whoever was
tormenting her. She'd have to stay and fight that
through. She couldn't bear to uproot herself even one
more time. It was the subconscious truth behind why
she had canceled that first doctor's appointment, and
why she hadn't raced off to Laredo the minute Molly
Gates had left her apartment yesterday. Deep down,
she didn't want to go.

So she'd stay and she'd face the music. Looking
around at Sam's family last night, she'd known for
sure that she couldn't do anything else.

All the people and the laughter had been in such
harsh contrast to her own life that she'd had to wonder how different her life might have been with a few
nips and tucks. Had her mother ever told her father
that she was pregnant? If the man had known he was
a father, would he have come for her when her great-
aunt died, or even before? She needed to know that
her child would be absorbed by Sam's incredible
family if anything happened to her. Surely if they
were aware of the child, the Walters family would
take him in. Sam's siblings were as passionate about
life as he was, and they let their hearts rip. His parents were steady, rock solid, the salt of the earth.

For the sake of her child, she had to come clean

with Sam. For the sake of herself, she couldn't keep living a lie. And for Sam's sake, he had to know, whether he hated the truth or not. She loved him, she thought weakly. She loved him too much to rob him of having a choice about what he wanted to do with the situation. She knew what it was not to have any choices. Her entire youth had been spent like that.

She let out another big sigh and sat back in her seat. Then it happened as she'd known it inevitably would. Someone approached her table.

Cait looked up as a shadow fell across the Formica. It was the cafeteria worker. What was her name? Holly Sinclair?

"You look glum this morning," Holly said.

Cait dredged up a smile. "Just thinking."

"Well, don't get so lost in thought that you forget what's good for that baby of yours. You shouldn't be drinking tea. I'll go put on a pot of decaf coffee for you."

"No, I don't like cof—"

Cait broke off.

She stared at Holly as the woman headed back behind the counter again. *That baby of yours.*

Cait felt her blood run cold. The cafeteria worker knew she was pregnant.

Her heart started clubbing her chest. Two days ago she would have wondered if she'd actually heard that or had imagined it. Now her stomach heaved, and Cait shoved to her feet. How? How could this woman know?

Maybe whoever had put that note in her locker had told her, had spread the word. But who? Who was it? She had to know.

Cait ran for the counter to go after her.

* * *

Tabitha and Jake stood staring around room 19 at the Shady Day Motel.

"This isn't good, is it?" Tabitha said eventually.

"Not even a little bit."

The room was unused. Empty. If not for its decrepit air and the dust coating almost everything, it would have looked as though it was ready for the next guests to check in. Jake made a move toward the door again and Tabitha hurried after him.

They went back to the front desk. A skeletal young woman with overbleached hair was chewing gum behind the counter and watching a black-and-white TV off in one corner. "Where's the occupant of room 19?" Jake demanded.

The woman shrugged without taking her eyes from the television. "How should I know? Tell you the truth, I never seen her."

"Never?"

"Guess she comes and goes at night. I work days."

"So who would have met her?" Jake pressed.

"The other guy. Jimmy Su. He works nights."

"Where can I find him?"

"I don't know where he lives."

"Look it up."

The woman finally glanced away from the TV, startled by his tone. "Yeah, all right. Is this important?"

"Very." She knew he was a police detective from Mission Creek. He'd had to flash his badge to get her to open the room. Irritated, Jake watched her go into a back room and called after her, "Get me a phone number, too, if you have one."

Tabitha pressed her fingers to her mouth. She was pale. "You're going to call this Jimmy guy?"

"If I can. It'll cut down on time. What was Cait doing today? Do you know where she is?"

"I think she's been staying with Sam. She hasn't been home much."

Jake took his cell phone from his belt and handed it to her. "Call there. Make sure she's with him."

"What do I tell her?"

"That in all likelihood, Deena Hines is in Mission Creek. Somewhere. Tell her and Sam to step up their guard."

The desk clerk came back with an address and phone number written on a slip of paper. Jake reached over the counter and grabbed the phone there. He brought it up onto the counter and punched in the number. When a groggy voice answered, Jake identified himself.

"Hey, man, what's this about? I didn't do nothing. I been sleeping since I got home at six."

"This isn't about you," Jake growled. The cop in him wondered what might have prompted Jimmy Su's remark, but he had no time for it now. "Tell me about the guest in room 19 at the Shady Day."

"What'd she do?"

"Tell me."

"Not much to tell, man. I hardly ever see her. She like turns up once a week and just stays for a coupla hours. Then she goes again. Pays good, though. She's had the room for like three weeks."

Since Sam and Cait had been rescued and Hines was put away, Jake thought. "What's she look like?"

"Kinda skinny, if you ask me. Short hair. Kinda brown. I don't remember too much else."

"If someone brings you a picture this afternoon, think you can ID her even if her hair looks different?"

"Maybe. Probably."

"Okay, then. When a police officer knocks on your door later, don't run and don't shoot."

"Why would I do that?"

"I don't know. You tell me." Jake hung up the phone. He looked at Tabitha. "Well?"

"No one's home," she said. "Not at Sam's place or at Cait's. I had to call the hospital to get Sam's number, so I'm having them check to see if they're around. Maybe there was an emergency and Sam got called in."

"Good thinking."

"Deena Hines," Tabitha breathed. "I don't believe it."

"We don't have anything concrete yet," Jake cautioned her. "But I don't like the looks of this at all."

"Nobody's seen Deena in Mission Creek, have they?"

"No, but I think Deena had long hair. Maybe she cut it all off and colored it. Maybe she wears a wig. We'll know if this Jimmy Su can identify a picture. She's just been using this place as a red herring, letting everyone believe she left the area. Why go to all that trouble unless she's been in Mission Creek all along, up to no good?"

"I don't know," Tabitha said helplessly.

"We're about to find out. Let's go."

* * *

Cait ducked around the counter and paused there. "Holly?"

There was no answer from the back room. Cait looked over her shoulder. Everyone in the cafeteria was staring at her. Small wonder. She plunged onward, through the door into the kitchen.

"Holly, I need to ask—" Cait broke off. "What are you doing? That's not coffee."

The woman's head jerked up as she poured some white powder into the machine. Her eyes glinted, and a feeling of horror sped clear to Cait's soul.

Something was wrong here. Something was very wrong.

Cait cleared her throat. "How did you know?" she asked hoarsely. "About my baby?"

Holly didn't answer. She gave a howl of frustration and grabbed for something on the counter where she was working. Cait couldn't see what it was. It was hidden behind another bag of coffee. Then Holly lifted it and Cait felt her legs start to fold.

It was a gun.

She shook her head helplessly. "I...I don't understand."

"Because you're stupid!" Holly screeched. "Why did you have to come back here?"

Cait was lost. "Back where?"

"To the kitchen. Damn it, this changes everything!" The gun in her hand wobbled. "From the very beginning, you've messed with everything!"

Cait looked from the gun to the white powder again. "What are you doing with that? What is it?"

"It would have taken out this whole stupid hospital and all you perfect people in it!"

Holly's gaze swung wildly about. That terrified Cait most of all. Then some of the mist of confusion in her brain cleared. And she had one sharp thought that turned her limbs to stone.

Her baby. If this woman shot her, her baby would surely die.

No! She had to think. She pressed her fingers to her temples.

Holly screamed again. "Keep your hands down!"

Cait dropped them fast. "Please. You've got to calm down."

"Why? Tell me one good reason why! You people ruined my whole life!"

"I don't even know you!" Cait cried.

"Yes, you do! You do!"

"No, I—"

"*Shut up!* Shut up or I'll shoot you!"

Cait shut up. And prayed.

Could anyone out in the cafeteria hear this? They'd all seen her come back here. But there was always a buzz of conversation in that room. Unless someone was specifically listening, she couldn't be sure Holly's shouts would be overheard.

Holly was fumbling with the powder, still trying to pour it into the coffeemaker without taking the gun away from Cait's direction.

Cait understood what Holly planned to do. Poison everyone who drank that coffee. Then kill her because she knew.

Someone in the cafeteria would surely hear the

gunshot, she thought wildly. But then it would be too late.

"Get away from that door," Holly yelled suddenly. "I'm not going to let you run."

Cait quickly took a step forward and to the side, keeping her back against the wall. Then she felt a knob dig into her skin between her shoulder blades. She started to look over her shoulder, but Holly waved the gun at her. "Don't move. Just stay there. I'm almost done here. Then I'll take care of you. That's what I'll do. I'll fix this coffee, then I'll take care of you."

No, you won't. Cait was shaking, but she'd realized what that knob was. It was the hospital intercom. The loudspeaker.

She had to get Holly to look away so she could turn it on. If she could turn it on and if she screamed, then everyone in the hospital would hear this, not just those in the cafeteria.

Sam. Sam was out there somewhere. Unless he'd gone outside with Gil and his family. Please, God, she prayed, don't let him have gone outside.

Cait stared at a spot on the far wall. She did it for so long while Holly started the coffee brewing that her eyes began to go dry and hurt. She was afraid to blink, afraid that even that motion would set the woman off. She stared until her head pounded, then, finally, Holly followed her gaze.

Cait used the moment to reach behind her quickly. She twisted the knob to full volume and she screamed.

"Hey!" Holly twisted around again violently. "What are you doing?"

Cait dove for cover behind a metal food cart just as the woman brought the gun up again and fired.

Sam was just stepping back into the lobby after seeing Gil off when a scream rent the air. For a crazy moment he only frowned and looked up at the ceiling, wondering where it had come from. Then he recognized the voice.

Cait. It was the same scream he'd heard the night Tabitha and Jake had rescued them.

The sound speared through him like a laser, shattering every plan he had ever made, anything he ever thought he knew about himself. He was going to lose her. Something was horribly wrong. He would lose her this time, and nothing else would ever matter again, nothing else in the world.

He started running, then skidded to a stop just as security officers fumbled for their weapons, and personnel and visitors all started talking at once, trying to figure out what was going on. A crashing metal sound filled the air. It finally dawned on Sam that he was listening to the hospital loudspeaker.

He had no idea where Cait was, but the intercom was on there.

Someone in the main office would know. The location would be lit up on the sound system. He couldn't wait that long. She needed him.

He remembered her telling him she wanted a cup of tea, so he ran for the cafeteria. Halfway there, more sounds filled the air. Another woman's voice, ranting, screaming, crying.

"I *hate* you!"

There was no answer, no response from Cait. Sam's heart froze, but he kept running.

"And Jake! And that bitch he's marrying! And your cat! I hate all of you who did this!"

Sam almost stumbled a little. Jake, Tabitha and Billy the Kid? What did that odd mix have to do with anything? Then understanding hit him hard.

"You destroyed my life when Branson went to jail!" the voice howled. "Look at me! *Look at me!* With some stupid, minimum-wage job while you all live your perfect little lives, and mine and Branson's just keep going down the toilet! And all because I couldn't get pregnant! I'm going to kill you and your precious little baby first, then I'll get all the others! You'll pay for what you did! I'll make you!"

Sam reached the cafeteria door, then he stopped, stunned. Your precious little baby?

Images fast-forwarded through his mind, faster and faster, but all as clear and concise as if they were actually playing out in front of his eyes all over again. Cait in that restaurant, declaring that she didn't drink anymore. Cait digging into food as though she'd just come off a hunger strike. Cait shrugging off his concerns about protection when they'd made love. Cait insisting that she needed a weekday off to do "errands."

She'd never told him. He was going to kill her as soon as he saved her.

But first he was going to take apart the crazy woman who thought she was going to rob him of the woman he loved and their unborn child. Sam ran again. This time, unlike the ordeal when they

were abducted, there was no semblance of sanity in
his mind.

No one stopped him. He shoved people aside and
went in the direction they were staring, the cafeteria
counter. He pushed past them and ran into the kitchen
at the back.

He had a split second—a heartbeat—to take in the
scene. Cait was on the floor behind some sort of
wheeled cart, moving it back and forth to keep it
between her and the cafeteria worker who'd been so
chatty with him earlier in the week. Holly somebody
or other. But he knew now that her name wasn't
Holly.

He made a roaring sound and went after her. She
looked his way sharply and brought the gun away
from Cait's cart. Then she fired.

The report was deafening. Sam never felt a thing.
He lunged forward and tackled Deena Hines.

The woman crumpled and went down under his
weight. She made a sound like all the demons in hell
being spewed out from her throat. He rolled with her
and found her hair in his hand.

A wig. He threw it aside.

She beat at him with her fists, fumbling, ineffectual
blows. "I stayed here to make you all pay!" she
sobbed.

Sam gritted his teeth and fought to restrain her.
"Yeah, we all caught that part."

"I was going to make you fall in love with me."

That startled him so much he almost lost his grip
on her. "Too late. I'm already in love with someone
else."

"If you had loved me, you would have given me

a life. It would have been even better than with Branson.''

He was finally able to pin her hands to the floor. ''Cait, call the police!''

''Who do you love?'' Cait croaked.

''You. Now call the police!''

''I love you, too.''

He felt himself grinning even with the writhing woman beneath him. ''Glad to hear it. Now get someone to take this woman off my hands so I can yell at you for not telling me you were pregnant.'' Deena brought her knee up. Sam swore and evaded it. ''Now!'' He heard Cait run.

''You live because she lives,'' Sam told her. ''It's as simple as that. Why did you go after Cait, damn it?'' He shook her a little. ''Why Cait?''

The woman twisted her head back and forth. ''She was just one of you. Then I found out about the baby. I saw...I saw the pregnancy test in her trash.''

She was the one who'd broken in. For the first time Sam noticed the long scratch down her forearm. So Billy had made her pay for it.

''Then I thought if she was crazy enough, I could get the baby and it would be mine.''

Everything inside Sam tightened. It took all his control not to hurt her. ''Over my dead body.''

''I would have had a baby! It didn't matter if I couldn't have you! We'd get Branson out of jail and we'd be a family! That's what I told him on the phone when I taped his voice!''

Sam remembered that the woman's inability to conceive was what had finally pushed Hines over the edge, aiming his fury at the hospital and its new maternity wing.

The woman was deranged, Sam thought just as he heard another voice shout behind him. He eased aside a little as a pair of female hands reached past him for Deena Hines. He looked up and recognized Molly Gates from previous encounters with her at the hospital.

"Jake just called me to be on the lookout for her," the detective said, twisting the woman's wrists together to throw handcuffs on her. "But I didn't think it would be this easy to find her."

When Deena was contained, Sam sat up. "Where's Cait?" he asked hoarsely.

"You mean the heroine of the hour?" She grinned. "Holding court out there in the cafeteria."

Sam stood and went that way on unsteady legs.

He found her at a table, encircled by a crowd. Sam pushed through them. "Excuse me. I need a moment with Super Mom here."

Her eyes, stricken and swimming, flew to his. "I'm sorry."

He hunkered down in front of her. "Just out of curiosity, when were you going to tell me?"

"Today." Her voice was a wretched whisper, and she felt as if she couldn't breathe.

She watched as he appeared to think about that, then nod. "Okay," he said, "here's the thing. I'm done trying to prove that I'm not the kind of man who won't make you crazy."

Cait's heart turned to stone. He was dumping her.

"It didn't work, anyway, and I'm not giving up Houdini. All I can give you is my love and a vow that I'll always take care of you and this baby, even if occasionally it's by some unorthodox means."

She felt her eyes widen. "What are you saying?" she breathed.

"I'm asking you to marry me." He looked affronted that she hadn't understood that.

Cait shook her head fast and hard. "No."

"No? I love you, and you said you loved me!"

"I do. I know. It's just…" How could she say it? "You'll get bored. I won't do that to you."

He stared at her for a moment, then to her amazement he laughed. "Not likely."

"You said—"

"I know what I said. I got bored with Nancy. But it finally dawned on me when we were watching my parents last night that if I never gave my best to Nancy, if I couldn't sustain things with Nancy, it was actually because I never had what they have. I never really loved her." He paused. "Plus, this whole thing with Hines has sort of reshaped my priorities."

"Yes," she whispered.

"Yes? You'll marry me?"

But Cait shook her head again. "No, I meant it reshaped mine, too. And this time when a gun was aimed at me, I did something to save myself."

He grinned. "Too bad there were no pipes in that ceiling back in the kitchen. I never did get to see you fly through the air."

Cait smiled shakily. Somehow she knew, without even talking to Jared, that this latest nightmare had finally and fully restored her to herself. No one could get through life without ever being a victim, without ever losing all control over things, but at least this time she had fought back.

Yes, she thought, she was restored. But she knew she would never be quite the same old Cait again. Because she had learned that her precious control was never foolproof and had only left her feeling isolated and alone.

She was also very tired of being polite and meek all the time, she decided. She reached out and grabbed Sam's collar to pull him close.

"Yes. I'll marry you. But that dog has to learn some manners."

Then she kissed him. Hard. The onlookers cheered.

* * * * *

Don't miss the continuation of the
LONE STAR COUNTRY CLUB:
Coming from
Silhouette Desire
in June, July and August 2003

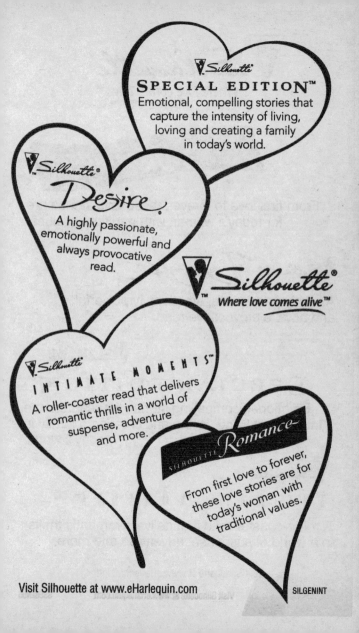

Where love comes alive™

From first love to forever, these love stories are
for today's woman with traditional values.

A highly passionate, emotionally powerful
and always provocative read.

SPECIAL EDITION™

Emotional, compelling stories that capture the
intensity of living, loving and creating a family in
today's world.

INTIMATE MOMENTS™

A roller-coaster read that delivers romantic thrills
in a world of suspense, adventure and more.